No...
Har...
ro...
by Ann...
come...
on the movie screen

starring
KEIR DULLEA · SUSAN PENHALIGON

Leopard in the Snow

Guest Stars
KENNETH MORE · BILLIE WHITELAW

featuring GORDON THOMSON as MICHAEL
and JEREMY KEMP as BOLT

Produced by JOHN QUESTED and CHRIS HARROP
Screenplay by ANNE MATHER and JILL HYEM
Directed by GERRY O'HARA

An Anglo-Canadian Co-Production

OTHER
Harlequin Romances
by REBECCA STRATTON

Many of these titles are available at your local bookseller
or through the Harlequin Reader Service.

For a free catalogue listing all available Harlequin Romances,
send your name and address to:

HARLEQUIN READER SERVICE,
M.P.O. Box 707, Niagara Falls, N.Y. 14302
Canadian address: Stratford, Ontario, Canada N5A 6W4

or use order coupon at back of books.

The Velvet Glove

by

REBECCA STRATTON

Harlequin Books

TORONTO • LONDON • NEW YORK • AMSTERDAM • SYDNEY

Original hardcover edition published in 1977
by Mills & Boon Limited

ISBN 0-373-02141-0

Harlequin edition published February 1978

PRINTED IN U.S.A.

CHAPTER ONE

LAURETTE often despaired of ever doing anything which had Nuri's wholehearted approval. Even if she thought right back to when their paths had first crossed, she could not recall a single occasion on which he had viewed her with anything more encouraging than a look of resignation, and more often, much more often, she earned a look of stern disapproval.

It had to do with her not being Turkish, she suspected, and also with the fact that her busy father had perhaps not given as much time as he might have done to teaching her what Nuri would consider were feminine attributes. She had to some extent run wild, she had to admit, but she had had a happy and uninhibited childhood and she regretted none of it.

The problem was that so much freedom had instilled in her a fiercely independent and outgoing attitude that, to Nuri at least, was very definitely unfeminine, and during the past eight years, while she had been in the benevolent but strictly traditional care of the Kayaman family, he had made no secret of his disapproval.

Her father, Angus Kearn, had spent a number of years in Cyprus with the British army, and had liked it so much that he vowed one day to return there. The opportunity arose rather sooner than he could have anticipated and in very unhappy circumstances, for only months after he left the forces his beloved wife was killed in an accident.

5

Heartbroken and unable to settle, he had eventually taken his little daughter and gone back to Cyprus. He had no experience of running a hotel, but he was a hard-working man and a pleasant and outgoing one, and his venture as a hotelier thrived until, within a few years, he was a quite successful man, though still a lonely one.

His loneliness was something he managed to conceal from everyone, except perhaps his growing daughter, for he was a man who made many friends, and his closest friend, rather surprisingly to some, was another ex-army officer. Refik Kayaman had been commissioned in the Turkish army until he returned to become head of the family export business, and it was perhaps the mutual memories of army comradeship that initially drew the two such different men together.

It had been a curious friendship in a way, for apart from their army experience the two men had little in common—the Scot, a big, red-haired man, naturally boisterous even in his latter years, moderately cultured, though with no pretensions to studiousness, and the Turk, dark, serious and steeped in the culture and customs of his race. And yet the two men had become such excellent friends that, apart from Laurette who adored him, when Angus Kearn died it was Refik Kayaman who mourned him most.

Refik Kayaman's wife was a Greek woman and his three daughters all took after her, with huge, softly innocent eyes and light skins, for they seldom exposed themselves to the sun as Laurette had done since childhood. They were all older than Laurette, but she got along well with the whole family, except possibly Nuri, Refik Kayaman's son.

Angus Kearn had had no relatives apart from some unknown cousins somewhere in Scotland who probably did not even know of his existence, so that when he died Laurette, at thirteen years old, had found herself virtually alone in the world. It had been a natural thing to do for Refik Kayaman to take her into his house and the care of his wife and daughters.

By then the two older daughters were on the brink of marrying and so Laurette became the close companion of Halet, the youngest, and their friendship had in many ways the same curious blending of opposites that had characterised their fathers'. Laurette was with people she knew and liked, and it had taken away some of the pain of losing her father—there was someone she could turn to.

Refik Kayaman had seen to it that she finished her education with three years at a school in Europe, but she had always come back during holidays to the Kayaman home and found a welcome there. It was an arrangement that suited everyone well, with the possible exception of Nuri, who saw her as an undesirable influence on his sister.

Laurette had wept as bitterly as any of the Kayaman daughters when Madame Kayaman died three years ago, and there had been no question of her doing other than go with the family to Turkey only shortly afterwards, when Refik Kayaman returned to his homeland, a fact that she sometimes suspected had been against Nuri's wishes—he had probably hoped she would stay behind.

Laurette had inherited her father's bright, outgoing nature as well as his copper-red hair and blue eyes, and she sometimes felt that even her colouring contributed to Nuri's disapproval. He had always been much less tolerant towards her than his father was, for possibly the older man saw in her a reflection of his old friend, and made allowances accordingly; overlooking things

7

that he would not have countenanced in his own daughters' behaviour.

Those three years at school in Europe had taken the more hoydenish edges off Laurette's liveliness and given her a veneer of sophistication, but to Nuri, even after eight years of knowing her as part of his family, she was still a wild redhead who could and did arouse his not inconsiderable temper all too frequently. He sometimes claimed he did not understand her, which was probably true, but she often wished he would try harder.

She wondered if he would have approved of her more if she spoke his language. After so many years of living in Turkey and in close proximity with Turkish people she probably should have made more of an effort, but the whole Kayaman family spoke such excellent English that she had never been obliged to learn in order to be able to converse with them. It had started, she supposed, when she first came to them very young and very bewildered, and in kindness they had used her language and never lost the habit.

At the English school in Switzerland she had learned a smattering of French, but that language too she had not really bothered to absorb to any degree of fluency. In fact she had had a very comfortable and undemanding existence since her teenage years, and all of it due to the kindness and generosity of her father's old friend and his family.

At twenty-one years old she was everything her father could have wished her to be. Petite, like her mother had been, and with a very feminine figure, she had a small heart-shaped face below her mass of silky-soft copper-red hair. Thick brown lashes surrounded her deep blue eyes, and her mouth was generously full and smiled a lot—she had no reason not to smile, except when Nuri was being unreasonable, like now.

She attracted enough male attention to make her more or less indifferent to Nuri's attitude of cool detachment—at least she often told herself she was. As she looked at him now through her thick lashes, the expression on her small face was quite unconsciously provoking. She would much rather have been on the same easy terms with Nuri as she was with his sisters and his father, but she had no intention of changing her entire character to achieve it, and he had given the impression that nothing less would do.

As he was his father's only son, it was to Refik Kayaman's sorrow that Nuri had not yet married and had a family of his own. The Turks set great store by family life and there had been opportunities in plenty, but Nuri was seemingly so involved with the family business now that his father had relinquished the reins to him that he appeared to have time for little else.

His sisters, and particularly the two who were married, sometimes teased him gently about it, but he seldom did anything more than smile, and completely ignored their suggestions that he should take this or that eligible young woman for his wife. He had never, at least never within Laurette's hearing, yet deigned to make a verbal reply, or give a hint of his feelings in the matter.

At thirty-three years old, he showed far more evidence of his father's Turkish blood than any of his sisters did. He was, Laurette supposed, an attractive man if one liked dark, brooding, hawk-like men, with the ability to induce shivers down the spine when he lost his temper.

He was tall, as his father was, lean and rangy but as strong as steel, as she had reason to know, and he had long legs that had on more than one occasion in the

9

old days brought him striding in pursuit of her and Halet when Laurette had led the two of them on some expedition of which he did not approve. He had never, to her knowledge, betrayed them to his father.

His eyes were black and could glitter like chips of jet below the thick raven's wing of black hair that more often than not fell across his forehead, as it did now, and somehow the light business suit he was wearing only added to the darkly primitive look of him. His skin gleamed like dusky gold above the white collar of his shirt, and in some of her wilder fancies Laurette imagined how much more at home he would look in the old traditional Turkish costume and surrounded by a harem.

His mouth was set firm as he looked across at her from beside the window, and the worst of it was that so far he had said very little. He simply stood and looked across at her with the harsh sunlight from outside diffused and softened and casting shadows across his arrogantly chiselled features so that she shifted again uneasily. However unwillingly she admitted it, he could make her feel incredibly gauche and uneasy simply by being silent, and she wondered if he realised it.

'You think I'm an awful brat, don't you, Nuri?'

She always found herself adopting a defensive and slightly challenging attitude with him, and sometimes wished she could appear more cool and sophisticated so that she could defy him without feeling like a bad-tempered child defying authority. Somehow that steady, glittering black gaze always made her feel that way.

'I think that you would have benefited from more discipline and less indulgence during your formative years, if that is the meaning of your question.'

He always spoke such pedantic English—not be-

10

cause he did not have a full command of the language, but because he disliked her penchant for using slang phrases and words which he considered unsuitable for a young woman to use. Unfortunately the result had more often than not been to make her use slang and smart-alec quips that she would not normally have used.

Once, just before Laurette left for school in Europe, he had reprimanded his youngest sister for using some vaguely impudent catch-phrase she had learned from her, and when Laurette had turned on him and accused him of being a bully as well as several other undesirable things, he had slapped her.

It could still surprise her, even after all those years, that he had had the temerity to slap her, for it was the one and only time in her life that she could remember being struck in anger. She had cried bitterly, she recalled, but only after Nuri had gone and Halet had comforted her, and she wondered as she looked at him now if she had ever really forgiven that blow to her teenage pride.

The present confrontation had come about because she had taken out the boat; a motor launch that she had driven on more than one occasion before, though never unaccompanied as she had today. She would have made certain that Nuri never knew about it, but some young man in another launch had tried to impress her with his own prowess by performing manoeuvres back and forth across her bow. A small error of judgment and the boats had touched, fortunately with no more dire result than some slight damage to the young man's boat, but in swerving to avoid him, Laurette had capsized and been brought home soaking wet, while the capsized launch was towed in.

Dry and changed, she now sat on the fat cushions of

the huge ottoman, curled up like a kitten and smelling of Floris bath essence, her copper-red hair still slightly subdued by damp, and curling into little wisps on her neck. If only Nuri had not been home when she came back, or if Baba Refik *had* been there, she would not now be faced with this interrogation by Nuri—at least not immediately. The boat was generally considered to be his only because he used it more frequently than anyone else did, but in fact she felt sure his father would not have objected to her using it.

Curling her legs more tightly under her, she looked across at Nuri, almost resigned to crossing swords with him again. 'No harm was done to your boat, there's not even a scratch on the paintwork. When it's been dried out it will be as good as new, so you don't have to glare at me so balefully, Nuri!'

'You think I concern myself only with the boat? Do you not realise the danger of what you did?'

His attitude took her by surprise for a moment and she stared at him, her wide eyes curious. The idea of him being concerned about her had not even entered her head and she found it intriguing enough to muse on for a few seconds before she answered him.

'I only had a ducking, Nuri, that's all.' She wished she could better define his expression, but with his back to the light it was difficult. 'I wasn't hurt, not even a bruise.'

'Then you are very fortunate!' His firm deep voice left no doubt that he considered her stupid as well as fortunate, so she was not unprepared for his next dictum. 'You may not be so fortunate again, so you will not take out the launch on your own!'

'Oh, but why not? You know I'm perfectly well able to handle it on my own!'

'On the contrary it is clear that in certain circumstances you are *not*,' Nuri insisted, 'and you will not do so again. Do I make myself clear, Laurette?'

'Oh, perfectly!'

He appeared to ignore her sarcasm, which rather surprised her too, and turned back to the window again, presenting his broad back to her angry gaze. 'It needs only for some other young fool to try and impress you with his skill and you could easily be drowned or badly injured.'

'Well, drowning me would save you a great deal of aggravation, surely, wouldn't it?'

Her blue eyes were bright with anger, and yet she never really knew why she always got so angry with him. It had always been like this—a few moments together and they disagreed about something or other; usually something to do with the way she had behaved. Quite often she felt remorse afterwards, because basically she believed he cared for her well-being, but somehow she could never do anything about her response to him, and they quarrelled.

He turned back to her, regarding her for a moment or two steadily, the expression in his eyes hidden by thick black lashes that always somehow looked much too feminine for that craggily masculine face. 'I wish that you would not make such remarks when you know quite well just how silly they are, Laurette.' His voice had that flat, harsh timbre that she recognised as barely controlled anger, and she felt a faint flutter of something that she refused to admit was regret. 'I want your promise that you will not take out the launch again unless you have someone with you.'

'You, for instance?'

He inclined his head in agreement. 'I suppose it will have to be, since I do not consider Halet a suitable companion on such expeditions.'

13

'Poor Halet, I should think she'll be thankful when she's married to Hussein!'

She should not have said that, she realised it as soon as the words were out of her mouth, and she saw Nuri's dark frowning anger that seemed to touch her even from the other side of the room. 'You think that marriage automatically gives a woman freedom to do as she pleases? Do you imagine that Hussein will allow her to behave as she likes simply because she is no longer in her family's care?' He came across and stood close beside the ottoman, looking down at her with fierce black eyes. 'You do not know Turkish husbands, *kizum*!'

'I wasn't suggesting that she——'

'You were suggesting that my sister would be well rid of her family's authority, Laurette—I am not a fool! More specifically, I suspect, you think she will be well rid of *my* influence!'

'Don't yell at me, Nuri!' She felt oddly breathless suddenly and tried to find words to make him understand that she had not meant to start this disagreement, any more than she meant to start others—it just happened. 'I wasn't—getting at you, I just——' She shrugged helplessly and hugged her legs more closely up under her as she sat among the fat soft cushions. 'Oh, I don't know how to talk to you without us fighting!'

Surprisingly he said nothing for several seconds, but stood over her like a lean dark Nemesis, casting his shadow across her. 'You could try, if you really wanted to, Laurette.'

The timbre of his voice stirred something in her and she looked up at him swiftly, her eyes wide and questioning, darting over the dusky gold features searchingly, without quite knowing what she was searching for. 'It's difficult when I know you don't really approve

14

of me,' she ventured after a few seconds. 'You never have, have you, Nuri?'

'Approved?'

He savoured the word as if he was unsure of its meaning in this context, then shook his head, and Laurette watched him curiously. There was something unfamiliar about him in this instance, something vaguely disquieting, and when he spoke again it was as if he chose his words very carefully.

'It was rather like bringing a being from another world into our household when you arrived after your father's death. Even after all these years I cannot make myself believe that you are as one of my sisters, it is not possible for me. If you had been more like them, perhaps, quiet and obedient, I might have been able to look upon you as one of them, but——' He spread his large hands palms upward and heaved his shoulders in another shrug. 'As it is, you are so different that I find you too—disturbing.'

It was not at all the sort of thing she expected of Nuri, and it was probably the longest speech he had ever made to her, so that she said nothing for a moment or two but sat with her eyes downcast in a fair, though unconscious, imitation of his sisters, not knowing quite what to say or do.

His words lent themselves to several different interpretations, but the one that seemed most likely, coming from Nuri, was the one she found hardest to accept. It could be that he was telling her in a roundabout way that he would prefer it if she was to go, and no longer be part of their family, and when she looked up at him again there was a curiously childish appeal on her small face, and the uncertainty she felt showed in her eyes.

'Are you trying to tell me that you'd rather I wasn't

here, Nuri? That—that you want me to go?'

She could not believe that his father knew about his feelings or that he would condone his telling her how he felt, but even though it was only Nuri's opinion it gave her a cold and incredibly lost feeling to be made so suddenly aware of his feelings towards her.

For eight years she had known he did not altogether approve of her, but she had accepted it as something not to be taken seriously. Now—she felt a flutter of something like panic in her breast as she considered what to do. She was twenty-one years old and should be quite capable of looking after herself, but somehow leaving Baba Refik and this, her home, alarmed her more than she cared to admit.

She was so preoccupied with the prospect that she caught her breath audibly when Nuri dropped down beside her suddenly and sat with his elbows resting on his knees. His face was in profile to her so that she could see the strong, hawkish nose and the arrogant poise of his head, the thick black lashes that looked so much longer seen from the side. He did not look at her when he spoke either, and that was not like Nuri.

'Have you thought of how—unconventional your position will be in our home when Halet is no longer here, *küçük*?' He had never called her child before either, and she was not altogether sure that she liked it, though there was too much else on her mind at the moment to allow her to object to it.

It hadn't occurred to her at all until he pointed it out to her that there would be anything untoward about her position once Halet was gone, and it should have done, she supposed. The truth was she had become so accustomed to being part of the Kayaman family that she saw herself in no other light; but Nuri was right, of course. With Halet gone she would be a single young

16

woman living in a house alone with two single men, neither of whom was related to her.

'I—I hadn't thought of that,' she confessed, and her voice sounded so small and uncertain that Nuri turned to her swiftly and reached impulsively for one of her hands, holding it in his large and comforting one for a moment. 'I suppose it will be wrong, won't it, Nuri? I mean, no one will understand like we do—like Baba Refik and the girls.'

'You do not include me among those who understand?' Nuri asked in a quiet voice, and she hesitated a moment before she answered.

'I don't know. You have brought the subject up and —well, I thought perhaps you might see it as a good opportunity to get rid of me after eight years.' She laughed, slightly unsteadily because she had never before felt quite as she did at this moment. 'I suppose you've been pretty tolerant, in fact, when I think about it! You already had three sisters, and inflicting you with another, bossy redhaired one was asking a bit much of you, wasn't it?'

He let go her hand, though rather slowly, almost as if he was reluctant to do so, turning that chiselled profile to her once more. It was evident that he had decided not to commit himself on the matter of tolerating her presence for the past eight years.

'I am quite certain that both Latife and Bedia will be quite willing for you to stay with them until you marry.'

'Marry?'

She stared at him, his matter-of-fact statement bringing a hasty flush to her cheeks, and when he turned his head and looked at her again, she noticed that one black brow registered surprise at her reaction. 'Surely you anticipate marriage before very long?' he suggested.

17

'You are quite old enough, Laurette, and it is unthinkable that you should not have a husband to care for you.'

'But I don't *want* a husband!' She made the declaration firmly, though with a hint of breathlessness, and once more Nuri's black brows expressed surprise. 'At least, not yet—there's plenty of time to think about getting married.'

'If you were married the problem of what to do when Halet leaves us would not arise,' he pointed out with chilling reasonableness, and the old familiar feeling reared its head once more as she turned on him, challenging and defensive.

'It's a pretty drastic solution!'

His eyes were on her, steady and glitteringly dark, suggesting impatience, as if he found her objections incomprehensible. 'Do you dislike the idea of marriage so much?' he demanded, and Laurette's eyes blazed at him.

'Do *you*?'

Her knowledge of Turkish was limited, but even so she recognised curses when she heard them, and she thought for a moment that he was going to simply get up and go stalking off. Instead he got to his feet but he stood looking down at her in a way that would have routed a less fiercely independent spirit.

'It is your viewpoint that is in question at the moment—my marriage plans are my concern!'

'And mine are *my* concern!'

She found it impossible to sit there while he towered over her that way, for it suggested that he had the upper hand, and she would not concede that. So she got to her own feet and stood facing him, a small angry figure with copper-red hair and blazing eyes, trembling like a leaf with the tangled emotions that ran through her.

18

Nuri looked down at her still, but now she felt a little less overwhelmed by him, and she could see how hard he was fighting to control that fierce temper of his. 'Your marriage is the concern of your family, and since you have no close relatives of your own, you are counted as a member of this household, *kizum*—take care you remember that!'

'You've just gone to great pains to remind me that I'm *not*!'

Nuri's eyes were like black fire as he looked at her, his straight firm mouth taut with anger. 'You deliberately misunderstand me, Laurette! As far as my father is concerned you are his daughter and he will take the same interest in your settlement as he did with my sisters—we both shall!'

'And you really think you can marry me off? Just like that?' She tipped back her head and challenged him with her blue eyes, breathing short and angrily through slightly parted lips. 'To some rich American, I suppose, so that you'll be sure I go as far away as possible!'

At any other time she might have found his fury awesome. His big hands clenched tightly at his sides suggested that he might strike out at any moment, and he held his head high so that he looked at her down that arrogant and hawk-like nose. 'Better to a Turkish husband, you little vixen, so that he may beat some good manners into you!'

He came striding past her and was out of the room while she still fought to recover her breath, and she spun round at the moment when he closed the door behind him. He did not slam it as some men would have done, but closed it with a controlled quietness that was somehow even more suggestive of violence, and she heard her own breath expelled in a long sound like a sigh.

19

It was a surprise to Laurette sometimes to realise that she was much more at home in Turkey than she would be if she went back to Britain. She had spent most of her twenty-one years in Cyprus and Turkey and she was better acclimatised both to the pace of life and the hotter climate. Going to Britain now would be like going abroad for her, which seemed strange when she thought of how very British her father had always considered himself, even after all his years away.

She looked around the salon, where she sat on the ottoman again since Nuri had gone storming off and left her, and thought how much she would miss the house as well as the family if she was obliged to leave, as Nuri suggested she should.

It was a very Turkish room, and yet she felt very much at ease there, and it occurred to her for the first time that she was something of a contradictory character. While she had adapted willingly and easily to most things Turkish and actually loved the way of life, she still retained her right to be independent in her behaviour, and would brook no suggestion of control, especially not from someone she considered had no right to exert it.

She understood and liked the Turkish character while still herself remaining very British in her outlook on most things, and it was little wonder that Nuri found her too complex for him to understand. She was neither Turkish nor yet completely European, and any man could be forgiven for finding the mixture beyond his comprehension.

The house seemed quiet, and the big *salon* particularly so now that Nuri had left her—his forceful personality could seem to fill a room when he was in it, and she sat on the pile of big cushions hugging her knees to her chin. She needed time to think since Nuri

20

had presented her with the problem of her own future to solve.

The *salon* was restful; it was her favourite room, with its many mirrors reflecting stray glimmers of sunlight from outside and giving the room a softly luminous look. Brightly coloured hanging rugs on three of the walls softened and muffled it, giving one the impression of being in a large, luxurious nest furnished with countless fat and comfortable cushions, as well as a modern suite.

There were gilt ornaments in plenty decorating the niches and alcoves too, and standing on every small table, with exotic brass lamps hanging from the ornamented ceiling. The windows stood open to a blessedly cool breeze off the water, the shutters fastened back to prevent their obstructing even a breath of it. She didn't see how she could leave this beautiful home she had known for so many years, and yet the way Nuri presented it, there was little else she could do if the strictness of Turkish behaviour was to be observed.

She should have anticipated it when Halet's betrothal to Hussein was announced, of course, but somehow she had not yet looked beyond the excitement of the coming wedding in a few months' time. She and Halet had always been so close that it seemed impossible that the dearest of her foster-sisters was to be the means of her leaving her home.

Getting up from the cushions with the grace that long practice had taught her, she walked across to the windows where Nuri had stood and, like him, stood looking out at the gardens. It was peaceful and beautiful and it did not seem possible that soon she must go and leave it. Perhaps she could get somewhere for herself not too far away, where she could still see Baba Refik and the girls—and Nuri too, she supposed; she would miss him as well, she had to admit.

'Laurette?'

She turned swiftly to see Halet coming in to the room, and smiled at her affectionately. She would miss Halet very much. Although she was a year or two older than Laurette, she had always seemed to take the role of younger sister. It probably had something to do with the fact that she was much less venturesome and always less sure of herself.

She was pretty, as her two sisters were, with a soft voice and a graceful way of walking that drew attention from a slightly ungainly figure. Both Latife and Bedia were now frankly plump after two children each, and undoubtedly Halet would be too in a couple of years' time, but she was charming and very feminine and Laurette thought she possibly loved her more than she would have done a true sister, for there had never been any jealousy between them.

'I thought you were being scolded by Nuri,' Halet confided, 'so I thought it best to stay away until he was gone.' Her innocent-looking dark eyes looked at Laurette curiously. 'Did I hear him go upstairs a moment ago sounding very angry?' she ventured, and Laurette pulled a wry face.

'We quarrelled—as always.'

Halet sighed deeply and shook her head. 'I do wish that you and Nuri could be better friends—it is such a pity.' She looked at her once more with that innocent curiosity in her eyes. 'What did you fight about this time, Laurette?'

'My getting married, of all things!'

'Oh, Laurette!' Halet took her hands, holding them tightly in her excitement. 'You are to be married also? Who is it? When is it to be?'

'No, no, no!' Laurette laughed as she stemmed the tide of excitement, and noticed Halet's look of disappointment. 'It was just a remark of Nuri's—he thinks I should be married and I think it's my concern when and if I marry.'

'If?' Halet looked concerned, her smooth brow wrinkling anxiously as she stood at the window beside her. 'But of course you will be married, Laurette, it is unthinkable that you would not be.'

'Which is precisely Nuri's sentiment,' Laurette remarked, and laughed again, a curiously uneasy sound that made Halet frown at her more curiously than ever. 'He's pointed out to me that I can't stay on here after you're married and gone, it wouldn't be right and proper—and he's right, of course. I just don't like his solution.'

It obviously hadn't occurred to Halet either and she looked quite distressed for a moment. 'Oh, but I am sure that Baba will not like you to go and leave him, Laurette.'

Shaking her head, serious for all she was half smiling, Laurette looked out of the window, letting the soft warm wind blow on to her cheeks. 'I don't want to leave him either, Halet, but, much as I hate to admit it, Nuri *is* right. I must find somewhere during the next few weeks.'

'You could come to Hussein and me,' Halet told her, then blinked in realisation when Laurette shook her head. 'Oh no, I suppose that is not a good idea.'

Laurette hugged her for a moment, grateful for her eagerness to take her in. 'I don't think Hussein would take kindly to the idea of sharing his bride so early in his marriage, do you?'

Halet blushed and shook her head, looking down at

her hands while she spoke. 'Is there no one that you would like to marry, Laurette?'

'Not at the moment.' Laurette watched the breeze stir among the pink tamarisk, and gazed into the distance without seeing anything at all. 'Sooner or later I shall fall in love with someone, I suppose, and then I'll marry him—if he asks me, of course, there's always that consideration.'

She smiled as she turned, but Halet was taking it all quite seriously. 'Oh, but of course he will want to marry you, Laurette! You are a very beautiful girl, many men will want to marry you.'

'One will do!' She smiled to let Halet know she was teasing her, then walked back into the room and sank down again on to the cushions of the ottoman, curling her legs up under her as she so often did. 'He'll probably have to get through one of Nuri's interrogations first too, so he'd better be pretty sure of himself!'

'Oh, Laurette!' Halet sat down beside her, her dark eyes so plainly troubled that Laurette wondered why she was taking it all so seriously. 'He means it only for your own good, you must know that—as he and Baba had the well-being and happiness of all of us at heart in the matter of marrying men who suit us. Latife and Bedia both love their husbands, and I could not wish for anyone but Hussein for my husband.'

'You love him, don't you, Halet?'

It was almost a plea, asking for confirmation that Halet was not simply making the best of what she had to do, but she need have had no doubts, for Halet's blushes were confirmation enough. She had seen them together too. Seen the way their eyes met and the way Halet's were hastily lowered, but not before they had passed the message that Hussein wanted to see. The way their hands would sometimes touch as if by acci-

24

dent, while Refik Kayaman's benevolent eye pretended not to see.

'Oh, yes,' Halet said softly, 'I love him. I wish that you could find someone to love as much, my sister.'

Laurette got to her feet again, curiously restless since that disturbing conversation with Nuri had put hitherto vague prospects to the forefront of her mind. She walked across to the window again and looked out, a strange fluttering sense of anticipation in her stomach.

'Oh, I will, one day,' she promised.

CHAPTER TWO

LAURETTE always enjoyed these gatherings, where her two familiar worlds mingled freely and she could feel at home in both of them. Furedin Ocak, Latife's husband, was a very social man and liked entertaining, a habit he had picked up while living in Europe for some years. They were always enjoyable, though rather more formal than she remembered her father's parties being, and the company was always well mixed.

This evening there was a German business friend and his wife, and a French student as well as one or two British acquaintances whom Furedin had met during the course of his work. He held a fairly responsible position with the Kayaman family firm, but he was much less traditionally minded than either his wife's father or her brother, though he got along well with both.

Halet and her fiancé were there too, although Laurette could not see them at the moment, and so was Nuri. It was a strange fact that Nuri often came with her when Latife and Furedin entertained and Laurette was invited. She had never yet determined why he decided to escort her when she was perfectly happy to go alone or with Halet and Hussein. Possibly it was simply because he had the Turkish dislike of a woman going anywhere unaccompanied where there was to be mixed company.

It was mostly to avoid Nuri that she had come outside, although he was an attractive enough escort to earn her the envious glances of the German businessman's plump and handsome wife. He had frowned over her taking another glass of *raki* when she had already had as much as she could sensibly cope with.

Inevitably they had disagreed about it, and a discreet but impassioned argument had ended when she walked off and left him, taking another drink as a gesture of defiance as she made her way to the garden door. In a way she knew she was seeking refuge as well as fresh air by coming out into the gardens, for her triumph was already turning sour, overshadowed by the knowledge that yet again she had quarrelled with him when there was no real cause to.

Latife and her husband had a house outside Antalya itself, built in the hills where the wind was cooler and the Bey mountains made a breathtaking backdrop to the fertile and beautiful countryside. The sea was near too, below steep, impressive cliffs that soared above sandy beaches and dropped shimmering falls of clear water from the mountains into the turquoise ocean.

The moon was a perfect Turkish crescent in a velvet dark sky and, combined with the scent of the magnolias that grew in profusion, it had a headying effect as she walked along the path from the house. Or perhaps it was not entirely the moon and the magnolias that made her feel so strangely lightheaded; maybe Nuri had been right and she should not have had that last glass of *raki*.

Her cheeks were slightly flushed, but the warmth in the *salon* could have accounted for that, and she was not yet prepared to admit that she was anywhere near as inebriated as Nuri's argument had implied—she was simply a little lightheaded, nothing more.

Leaning back against the trunk of one of the cypresses that rose like a row of black plumes against the

27

moonlit sky, she let the cool breeze blow across her fore-head, closing her eyes for a second or two to enjoy it to the full. The garden here was very much like the one around her foster-father's home, and just as delightfully quiet and peaceful, even with the chatter of voices coming from the crowded *salon*.

She wished she hadn't quarrelled with Nuri; but then she always regretted it, yet never managed to do any-thing about stopping herself before it happened. Of course Nuri was to blame for taking the initial action, but so often he was right and sensible in what he said, and that somehow made things worse. She sighed, gazing up at the moon and leaning back her head.

Her dress was made of soft cool silk, and when she spread her arms around the trunk of the tree and let the full sleeves fall like wings on either side of her, the breeze seemed to reach her whole body with its de-licious coolness. With her dress fluttering around her in the light wind, the moonlight gave her an ethereal look that was enchanting, the more so because she was unconscious of the fact.

'Hello!'

The voice came from some distance along the path from the house, and she dropped her arms, turning swiftly with her breath catching in her throat. Startled for a moment, her first thought was that Nuri had come in search of her and she was ready to offer the olive branch if he had. But it wasn't Nuri, and she looked rather vaguely at the man who stood on the path re-garding her with interest he made little effort to dis-guise. It was difficult to tell in the curious, indefinite blend of moonlight and artificial light from the house, but she thought he had hair that was almost as red as her own—a fact that he touched upon without hesi-tation when he spoke again.

'I spotted your red head some time ago.' He came along the path to join her, raising the glass he had in his hand in silent tribute before emptying it. 'I hope you speak English; I've been wondering all evening who you are. We redheads aren't very common around here, are we?'

'No. No, I suppose not.'

It was instinctive to glance over her shoulder for a sign of Nuri, although it annoyed her that she did it. Firmly bent on following up his advantage, the man stood his empty glass down on a convenient ledge and offered a hand; his smile wide and self-confident.

'Well, at least we speak the same language! It seems our host didn't get around to introducing us—I'm Ian Kearn; something in the civil service!'

For a moment the coincidence of their both having red hair as well as the same name struck Laurette as curious, and she was shaking her head as she took the proffered hand and shook it. 'How strange!' She laughed, withdrawing her hand when he seemed inclined to hold on to it for longer than was strictly necessary. 'My name is Kearn too—Laurette Kearn.'

He noted her unusual first name and raised a brow as he thrust one hand casually into a pocket. 'Laurette? I don't think I've come across that before; it's rather pretty.'

'My mother chose it.'

Bright, quizzical eyes speculated for a second. 'She must have known you'd grow up to be beautiful.' He laughed, a quiet, confident sound that suggested he was used to situations like this and enjoyed them. 'I could use the old line like—what's a lovely girl like you doing in a place like this, but after what I heard inside just now, it might not be discreet and then I'll have made a bad start. I'd hate to think I'd done that.'

Laurette was frowning, puzzled as well as trying to cope with a strangely fuzzy sensation in her head. 'I don't quite know what you heard. I——'

Ian Kearn glanced at the bright crowded room behind him and smiled. 'I thought I heard someone say that you were one of the Kayamans, but I couldn't see it somehow, not with those looks.'

Clear about one thing at least, she shook her head. 'Oh, but it's right in a way. You see, they *are* my foster-family.'

'Really?' He was plainly curious and making no secret of it. 'I find that very intriguing, Miss Kearn. Would I be indiscreet to ask how? Unless you married into the family.' He glanced quite openly at her naked left hand. 'And you're not married, are you, Miss Kearn?'

'Oh no, I'm not married!'

'Good!' He grinned amiably. 'That's a step in the right direction!'

His approach was something that Laurette had to confess she was not used to coping with. She was accustomed to admiration, open admiration in most cases, but Ian Kearn seemed so confident and sure of himself. He looked about twenty-nine or thirty years old, and was probably very successful with her own sex, even though he was in no way good-looking in the conventional sense.

'Are you an old friend of Furedin's, Mr Kearn, or do you know any of the rest of the family as well?'

She was seeking another subject in the hope of turning his interest, and from his smile he probably guessed it, but he was willing enough to go along with her for the moment, apparently. 'I've had brief contact with the formidable Nuri Bey, Miss Kearn, but I've never met anyone else. The charming Madame Ocak—Latife?—

I met for the first time this evening, and no one even mentioned that you existed.' The way he looked at her sent a little warning shiver along her spine. 'Which was very remiss of them.'

Her reaction was not even clear to herself in her present state, and she wished she had not had that extra drink, for she felt she needed, should have, all her wits about her in the present situation. 'Probably because I'm not a very important member,' she told him with a small and not very certain laugh. 'Being the youngest and a female as well.'

He pulled a wry mouth, his eyes curious. 'The Turkish outlook from you? Ah, but then you said you're part of the family, didn't you?' He smiled, persuasive and encouraging. 'I'm still intrigued by that situation, Miss Kearn.'

She had never been loth to tell anyone how good her foster-family had always been to her and she saw no reason to make an exception of Ian Kearn, even though he was a complete stranger to her. 'There's really no mystery about it. Mr Refik Kayaman and my father were very close friends, and when my father died he took me into his own family and cared for me, sent me to school. I've counted them my family ever since, and that's eight years now.'

'I see.' It was difficult to be certain if his eyes were blue in the deceptive light, but they speculated on her reaction quite frankly. 'And does that mean that you think of me as too—bold for coming out here especially to talk to you? Does that bother you?'

Intrigued, whatever else she felt about him, Laurette shook her head. 'I don't think so, Mr Kearn. I'm sure Latife and Furedin wouldn't have invited someone they couldn't trust to behave himself.'

He smiled, accepting the challenge without letting it

deter him in the least. 'Oh, don't worry about that, Miss Kearn, but I was thinking about what your—brother will think about me coming out to find you. I think he knew I was following you and I've half expected to find him breathing down my neck by now.'

'Oh no, he wouldn't——' She stopped short, knowing full well that Nuri would, if he thought there was any chance at all of her not being able to cope with her redhaired compatriot, come out and look for her himself. 'I don't think he'll bother.'

Ian Kearn eyed his empty glass as if he would like it refilled but was not prepared to leave her to achieve it. 'I saw the two of you in there earlier,' he confessed with a grin. 'You looked as if you might be having a difference of opinion. Or as if he was laying down the law.' The grin widened and became quizzical. 'I hear tell that Nuri Kayaman isn't a good man to cross.'

She felt oddly sensitive about Nuri suddenly, and the sensation both surprised and disturbed her, so that she walked away from him for a moment, trying to bring her reactions under control. Standing in the shadow of a huge magnolia that displayed its waxy blossoms in the moonlight and filled the air with heady scent, she was aware that the redhaired man was watching her.

Undoubtedly he was curious about Nuri, that hesitation before referring to him as her brother had brought a swift flush to her cheeks that she was at a loss to explain. He had thought Nuri was laying down the law, and she supposed he was right, but she wanted to let him know the reason for Nuri behaving as he had, and she wondered if he would understand.

Turning her head towards him, she spoke over her shoulder. 'I don't know how well you know Turkey, Mr Kearn——'

'Not very well yet, but I like what I've seen so far.'

'I'm sure you'll love it. It's a beautiful country and the people are among the kindest and most hospitable in the world, but they have a very—protective attitude towards their womenfolk.'

'So I understand.'

She pulled a magnolia from its bush and held it in both hands, inhaling its perfume for a moment. 'I'm just trying to show you why Nuri was—as you said—laying down the law. To Nuri I'm his youngest sister and he treats me accordingly.'

'I see!' Something in his tone suggested only partial belief in what she said, and she looked at him for a moment uncertainly. He had a rugged face rather than a handsome one, and it was certainly attractive when he smiled. 'Well, if I had a sister like you *I'd* keep an eye on her too!'

Laurette walked back to join him. He intrigued her, attracted her, she was ready to admit, and she twirled the magnolia in her fingers, shaking her head. 'Unfortunately I don't take kindly to having an eye kept on me,' she confessed, then added hastily in case he suspected she was under some kind of restraint, 'though I know it's done with my best interests at heart, and I try not to object too much as a rule.'

'But sometimes you do, like earlier?' He referred to her exchange with Nuri, obviously, and was probably making much more of it than was true.

She looked down at the waxy white blossom in her hand and pulled a face. 'We argued over a glass of *raki* —silly, isn't it? But Nuri thought I'd had enough, and the trouble is that he's nearly always right; that's what I find so maddening!'

Ian Kearn's eyes were more shrewd than she had realised and he was regarding her with a kind of narrow-eyed speculation that she found rather disturbing. 'I still can't quite get over finding a beautiful English redhead so firmly ensconced in a Turkish family.'

'Scottish.' She made the correction as automatically as her father had done so often in her hearing. 'My parents were Scottish, Mr Kearn. Daddy came out with the army to Cyprus, and he liked it so much that when my mother died and he was left alone he came out here, with me, and took over an hotel on the island. I've spent most of my life out here.'

'He was in the army, you say?'

She detected something different in his voice and looked at him curiously, although she had no objection to talking about her father. 'Originally yes, he joined as a boy when his own parents died. His name was Angus Kearn and he came from somewhere in Argyllshire, although when my mother was alive we lived in Surrey – I was born there, in fact.'

'And did he come from a little place called Ben Crochan, near Glencoe, by any chance?'

He was looking at her with a bright gleam in his eyes, a look of expectation, she thought, and wondered at the sense of sudden excitement she felt as he waited for her to answer. Swiftly she recalled her father's voice, recounting the stories of his own childhood in Scotland, a country he had left when he was little more than a schoolboy.

'That's right, I seem to remember it was Ben Crochan where he came from.' She looked at him, anxiously almost, yet half afraid for reasons she could not define. 'How could you know that?'

Ian Kearn was smiling; a broad, bright smile that showed how pleased he was with whatever he had to say. 'I guessed it because that's the village my own father came from originally, although like you I was born south of the border. He had a cousin called Angus Kearn who joined the army as a boy, when his parents died. It's a heck of a coincidence, you must admit!'

'I—I can't quite believe it.'

His excitement almost matched her own, and he was using his hands now to emphasise his words. 'Same name, same village, same red hair, my father was a red-head as well, and the fact that his cousin Angus joined the army as a boy too. Nobody heard anything of him for years and then there was something in the paper one day, it was donkey's years ago now, but I just about remember it.'

'He won the M.M. for gallantry, it was in all the papers! He had the cuttings, though he never would tell me about it, and it was not long after I was born.'

'Dad claimed it was his cousin Angus, but Mum wouldn't have it, she said both Angus and Kearn were both common enough names in Scotland. Dad kept the cutting, though, I found it when we were going through his things, he was so sure it was his cousin.' He pointed to her red hair and put a hand on his own and laughed. 'This would seem to clinch it, eh?'

Laurette wasn't quite sure what to feel apart from a kind of wild excitement at the idea of finding a cousin she had not even known existed. For so long now she had thought of herself as having no one else in the world but the Kayamans and it would take a bit of getting used to if it was true, and she saw no reason to doubt it. She looked at Ian Kearn and smiled a little vaguely, her head spinning more confusedly than ever.

It would take time to accept a complete stranger as someone with blood ties that made him closer to her than Baba Refik and the girls, and Nuri. It wasn't easy yet to accept it, and yet she somehow knew it was true. 'I—I suppose we're second cousins, is that right?'

Ian Kearn was still smiling, as if he had no doubts at all, and she wished she could share his obvious pleasure instead of feeling so stunned by it all. 'Oh, I think the coincidences are too much for it not to be right, don't you? There can't have been two Angus Kearns in a place as small as Ben Crochan! I went there once and it's little more than half a dozen houses and a kirk!' He took her hands and held them, then laughed suddenly and shook his head. 'I just can't get over discovering I have such a stunning cousin!'

'It's—unexpected.' She too laughed, but it was a small breathless flutter of sound, not nearly as confident as his. 'I can't quite believe it yet.'

His hands squeezed slightly and he smiled down at her with unmistakable meaning. 'Imagine—I can see you as often as I like, being your cousin, naturally, but you're not such a close relation that it makes——' He winked an eye. 'You know what I mean? Oh, I can widen your outlook, little cousin; take you around a bit and show you what the rest of the world looks like!'

His excitement was infectious, but only to a degree. Somewhere inside her Laurette felt a curious reluctance to have her safe and comforting little world shattered by this boisterous, self-confident man. She wanted to go on seeing him, as her cousin, but he was still too strange to her to make the idea of changing her whole way of life to suit him acceptable to her.

Maybe she had become more Turkish than she realised in the past few years since she came back from school, but she liked the pace and tempo of her present life. It was familiar and pleasant, and she was not at all sure that she wanted to fall in with Ian Kearn's plans for her as wholeheartedly as he obviously expected her to.

It was while she was still trying to come to terms with her own uncertainty that she saw Nuri coming from the house, his purposeful stride unmistakable as he headed in their direction and his dark face shadowed and unfathomable in the gentle light. Without quite knowing why, she welcomed his appearance almost gratefully.

Ian Kearn had seen him too, and he gave her a brief, quizzical glance before turning to look at Nuri, and she forgot for the moment that he had said they'd met before. Nuri's black eyes looked first at her, scanning her flushed face with a suggestion of suspicion.

Heaven knew what prompted her to do what she did, she had never been so familiar with him before, but she pushed her arm under his and looked up at him with a smile that made a provocative curve of her soft mouth. He was a strong and familiar presence and for some inexplicable reason she felt she needed his familiarity.

'You'll never guess what's happened, Nuri!' Her voice sounded light and breathless and she squeezed the arm she held, in defiance of the suddenly tensed muscles. Her tucking her arm through his would have taken him by surprise. 'I want you to meet Ian Kearn, something in the civil service, he says. Ian, my foster-brother, Nuri Kayaman!' Unaware of just how tightly she clung to him, she looked up at him, watching his face, waiting for his reaction. 'Nuri, would you believe that Ian is my second cousin?'

'I believe we have met on an earlier occasion, Mr Kearn.'

They shook hands and it all seemed so very civilised that, had she not seen the look in Nuri's eyes, she would have thought he simply accepted the fact without passing comment. But those black, glittering eyes were looking at Ian Kearn searchingly, noting the fresh open face, and the smart white dinner jacket that fitted broad muscular shoulders with almost the same perfection his own did.

With her hand still on his arm she could feel how taut and suspicious he was of the other man, no matter how polite he was being. 'I am rather puzzled by this reference to your being related to Laurette, however. It is rather an odd claim to make, surely.'

It was unlike him to refer to her by her first name when speaking to a stranger, and she blinked at him in surprise for a moment. 'Oh, but Mr Kearn didn't exactly make a claim, Nuri. He came out and we started talking, and then he——'

'*Lütfen*, Laurette; let Mr Kearn tell me about it, I am very interested. To suddenly find that you have a cousin must be quite a shock to you, but please—tell me about it, Mr Kearn.'

'But I can tell you just as well!'

Nuri ignored her, though he squeezed her hand lightly against his side with the pressure of his arm, and looked at Ian Kearn as if he suspected he would find the explanation difficult. His steady, black-eyed gaze was implacable while he waited for him to begin, and Laurette could well understand the brief, reticent glance her new-found cousin gave her before he spoke.

'I saw Miss Kearn come out here, that's how it all started, and thought I'd come out and have a word with her.'

'I noticed that you followed her out.'

His voice was quiet, not suggesting anything at all beyond the fact that he had seen him follow her, and Ian Kearn leaned himself casually against one of the cypresses, a hand in his pocket. 'It was the fact that we both had red hair—it's not a common sight in your country, you must admit.' He smiled at Laurette and managed to convey that the colour of her hair was not the only reason for his following her, though Nuri would know that well enough.

'It was when we started exchanging names and we got to the fact that Laurette's father was called Angus Kearn that the coin dropped. After that there were just too many coincidences for there to be any doubt that our two fathers had been cousins.' He listed the coincidences one by one on his fingers while Nuri watched and listened, his dark face betraying nothing of his reactions. 'Well—after all that there could be no doubt that we were—*are* second cousins, wouldn't you agree?'

'It has to be true, doesn't it, Nuri?' She was holding on to his arm and so far he had done nothing to discourage the unaccustomed familiarity. Indeed her hand was pressed close to his side in a way that seemed to suggest he was actually liking the situation. 'You can see that it must be right, can't you?'

'It would seem to be so.'

Nuri made the admission with such obvious reluctance that she could not quite understand him. He should surely have welcomed any possibility of her finding some of her own people, for it would mean that there was more than a chance of her taking up with them, perhaps even of her going to join them, which would solve the problem of what was to be done with her when Halet married.

Instead, the feeling that he was not at all pleased with the idea persisted, and when he looked down at her suddenly she felt a faint flutter of reaction in her heart as she waited for his next move. Was he going to suggest that she should get to know her own family as a prelude to her leaving his home? She tried to interpret what was in his eyes, but dark lashes formed an effective screen, and she could only wait.

'You are quite sure of it, are you not, Laurette?'

39

She glanced at Ian Kearn's pleasant, friendly face and wondered at her own hesitancy, then returned her gaze once more to Nuri. She did not want to deny that Ian Kearn was her cousin, but she wanted even less for Nuri to see it as an excuse to see the back of her; that troubled her more than she would have believed possible.

'Nuri, I believe it, I think Ian is my cousin, but— I'm wondering if——'

Strong fingers closed over hers in a gesture so unexpected that she caught her breath and glanced up again at that dark, unfathomable face. It was the second time in a few days that he had held her hand, and she tried not to remember that the last time had been when he was advising her to find herself another home. 'Surely you are pleased, *bebek*?'

This was a side of Nuri she did not remember having seen before, and she found it totally disarming. He might almost have been trying to impress Ian Kearn with their closeness, and she did not understand him at all. Strength and a kind of autocratic assurance were what she had come to expect of him, but not gentleness —not that deep softness in his voice. That was something she was neither prepared for nor accustomed to.

'Oh, but of course I am, Nuri, it's very exciting.'

The muscular arm still pressed her hand to his side and she tried hard to ignore its pressure—he was doing no more than lend his moral support. 'Then you will have much to talk about, hmm?'

'I—I imagine so, yes.'

Taking her hand, he removed it from his arm and held it for a moment before he let it go. 'Then I will leave you together to talk. I shall know where to find you when it is time to leave for home.'

His glance encompassed everything about Ian Kearn,

40

as if he meant to keep the picture of him in mind—his frankly curious face and his shorter, stockier figure in its smart dinner jacket, and the red hair that was the same copper colour as Laurette's but more wiry and lacking the same silky softness. If Ian Kearn had mischief in mind then that searching scrutiny would certainly have discouraged him.

'Mr Kearn.'

He gave a brief polite bow and left them, Laurette following his long-legged stride across the garden with that vague look of disbelief still in her eyes. It was Ian Kearn's voice that recalled her. 'Nice of him,' he said, and if it was sarcasm, she did not recognise it.

She pulled herself together hastily, putting Nuri to the back of her mind for the moment. 'I can't wait to tell Latife that she's unwittingly found me a cousin I didn't know I had.'

'You exchange confidences like true sisters, then?'

'Oh yes, of course.'

Ian Kearn took a cigarette from his case and lit it, then seemed to recall himself suddenly and reached for the case again. 'I'm sorry; do you smoke?'

'No, I don't, thank you. Baba Refik doesn't like it, so —we don't.'

'Just you girls?' He put the case back in his pocket and smiled at her quizzically. 'He's something of a traditionalist, like his son, isn't he?'

She did not like to have to defend her foster-father. It was true Refik Kayaman was a traditionalist, but she did not see it as a fault and she resented criticism of him. 'He's a wonderful man, a really wonderful and kind man. He smokes and so does Nuri, but if they prefer us girls not to then it's no great hardship.'

He was leaning against one of the trees and looking at her through the smoke from his cigarette, apparently intrigued by the idea of her being so compliant. 'It seems as if I've got a whole lot of things to learn about my new cousin, haven't I?' he suggested, and drew on the cigarette again deeply, narrowing his eyes against the rising smoke expelled from pursed lips. 'You're almost more Turkish than you are Scottish, it seems.'

It was something she was beginning to recognise with increasing frequency lately, and she admitted it without hesitation and with only a hint of defensiveness. 'I suppose I am in some ways, though you wouldn't get Nuri to agree with you! He still thinks of me as a heathenish redhead and thinks I need beating into shape!'

'Does he?' He studied the end of his cigarette for a second. 'That isn't the impression I got just now.'

'Oh, that was——' Laurette stopped hastily before she betrayed too much. For all he was her cousin, Ian Kearn was still a stranger and she could not bring herself to tell him that Nuri had never before behaved towards her as he had a few minutes ago. Instead she laughed and went off on another track. 'I suppose I am a bit too much for a conventional Turkish family sometimes, and Nuri usually lets me know it!'

Once more he studied the tip of his cigarette while he spoke, so that she wondered just what was going on in his mind behind that convenient smoke screen. 'Laurette, I know I've only just met you, and it's probably none of my business, but if that man—What I mean is if there's any pressure being brought on you to—to marry him or something, then you'd better come back with me to my hotel until we can see about sending you home to England.'

Too stunned to fully grasp what he had said for a moment, Laurette simply stared at him, her lips parted. 'Oh, you couldn't be more wrong!' She shook her head hastily to bring herself back to clear facts, but found it

42

incredibly difficult with such an idea in mind. 'Nuri would no more dream of marrying me than he would a—a—Oh, the very idea is ludicrous!'

'Is it?'

He asked it seriously, otherwise she might have laughed. Instead she blinked, still more uneasy. 'But of course it is! Nuri is a hard-headed businessman and if he marries anyone it will be some wealthy man's daughter—and either Turkish or Greek. His mother was Greek, you know, he's only half Turkish.' She looked at him with wide searching eyes for a second or two. 'I'm not being held against my will or anything half as dramatic as that; you really don't have to worry about that, though it's very nice of you to be so concerned.'

He seemed convinced and actually grinned somewhat sheepishly, as if his earlier dramatic suggestions embarrassed him. 'Well, you're my cousin, after all. I should be concerned about you, even if I have only known you a few minutes.'

'There's no need, I assure you. I wouldn't dream of leaving home—not yet anyway. Not until Halet gets married.'

'That's another of the Kayaman daughters, isn't it? I met her with her fiancé earlier.' Laurette nodded, and he looked at her curiously. 'And what happens when Halet gets married?'

She shrugged, walking off a few paces until she leaned against the same lofty cypress once more and gazed up at the moon. She didn't want to admit how insecure it made her feel, to know that her familiar and comforting world was going to have to change completely in less than two months' time.

'It's—difficult. You see, there'll only be Baba Refik and Nuri left when Halet goes, and—well, it just isn't the thing for me to stay on there with the two of them.'

'Ah, I see.'

'I shall have to find somewhere of my own.'

Her voice alone was enough to tell him how she felt about it, and he came and stood beside her, one hand on the tree she rested against, his eyes watching her closely. 'You really don't want to leave, do you?' he asked, and she wondered why he sounded so surprised.

She shook her head, not risking words yet, then she turned her head and caught a swift sight of him in the instant before he became distinct, shaking her head to clear it of the image she thought she had seen for a moment. The angle of his head and the bright red hair had given her a glimpse of someone she had once known better than anyone in the world, and it startled her for a second.

Then she laughed, a short and slightly unsteady sound. 'Just for a moment you looked exactly like Daddy, as I remember him. It's the red hair, of course, and the shape of the face and head.' She took a second to ponder on something that had only now become clear. 'It's awful,' she confessed, 'but I sometimes forget what he looked like.'

Ian Kearn was shaking his head, his mouth crooked into a smile as he rested his weight on the hand beside her on the tree. His eyes were darker now that his back was to the light, and he watched her steadily while he spoke. 'I hope you're not going to look upon me as a father substitute, Laurette,' he said quietly. 'That wasn't what I had in mind at all.'

It shouldn't have surprised her, of course, he had made his intention clear from the start, but somehow she could not quite understand her own reaction. She liked this new-found cousin very much, and in other circumstances she would not have minded in the least that he made his meaning unmistakable, but here, tonight, with Nuri only a call away, she felt curiously inhibited.

Her hasty glance over one shoulder told its own story, apparently, for Ian too looked in the same direction and his mouth showed a suggestion of a smile as he shook his head. 'It seems to me,' he remarked wryly, 'that Nuri Bey has already beaten you into shape, cousin!'

'Nothing of the sort!' she denied it swiftly, perhaps too swiftly, for Ian was smiling again. 'Ian, if you——'

'I want to kiss you, and since you're my cousin I don't see how anyone can object unless it's your Turkish —brother. Do you?'

She shook her head, wordlessly. Without a doubt Nuri would object, though only because he thought she would not be a willing partner, and she prayed fervently that he would not come out again just yet. Ian pivoted on the arm that supported him and put his other hand beside her head while he looked down at her for a second.

'You really are a beauty,' he said, and she saw him smile as he leaned closer. 'Hello, little cousin!'

His mouth was much more gentle than she expected somehow, and he let her go almost at once, though he kept his hands at either side of her and stood looking at her for a while longer before he bent his head over her again, this time drawing her into his arms and holding her mouth for much longer, so that she began to struggle, more by instinct than because she found his kiss repellent.

His eyes had a bright glowing look in the softness of moonlight and he looked dark rather than redhaired. One hand traced the shape of her face, brushing back the copper-red hair from her cheek and lingering like a caress against her neck. 'I'll see you again, won't I, Laurette?'

She nodded without stopping to think, then glanced up at him, her eyes shadowed by the long brown lashes that fringed them. 'I'd like to.'

He laughed softly and it made a warm breeze against her face. 'I suppose I'd better not come to the house for you, had I?'

'Why not?' She was being far too defensive, she realised, but she couldn't bear the thought of him thinking of her family as anything but kind and hospitable people. 'You'd come for me if we were in England, wouldn't you?'

Ian pulled a wry face at her. 'In England I shouldn't have to get past Nuri Kayaman!'

Laurette shook her head impatiently, pushing his arms away and walking past him, turning to face him again when she stood some distance off. 'You don't have to worry about Nuri—why should you?'

He was shaking his head, a small, crooked smile on his mouth. 'You may not have to worry about Nuri Kayaman, my lovely cousin, but you probably have him thoroughly tamed by now—for me it's different!'

'That's not true at all!' She could not admit that she had any influence at all on Nuri, certainly she did not have him as firmly under her will as Ian suggested, but suddenly the idea intrigued her. 'It's nonsense,' she told him.

Against the yellow light from the *salon* she saw Nuri and she watched as he came across the gardens towards them on his long easy stride, a curious and unfamiliar flutter of sensation in her stomach at the sight of him. Then, when he was almost upon them, she went to meet him and caught at his arm as she had earlier, feeling the muscles tense briefly as they had that first time, at the unfamiliar touch of her.

46

He did nothing about it, however, but looked across at Ian, then immediately again at her, his black eyes scanning swiftly over her flushed face. 'Are you ready to go home, Laurette?'

She smiled up at him, using her eyes in a way she would never have had the nerve to do normally, if Ian had not made that remark about her ability to influence him. 'Whenever you are, Nuri!' She looked back at Ian in a way she knew well was provocative as she could make it. 'Goodnight, Ian—if you want to see me, you know where I live, don't you? Don't be afraid to call.' She looked up at Nuri again through the thickness of her lashes, but did not quite meet his eyes.

He turned his head briefly and called a short but polite goodnight to Ian, and as they went towards the house she still had her hand tucked under his arm, looking up at him again and this time meeting the bright dark glitter in his eyes with a hint of defiance.

'Are you angry?' she asked, and he said something half under his breath in Turkish, something she thought it was as well she did not understand.

'I will not be used to provoke your men friends, Laurette! Don't ever do it again!'

The violence of his anger startled her and she looked up again anxiously. 'Oh but, Nuri, I only——'

'You used me, and I will not have it! If you wish to arouse the jealousy of your men friends you will find some other way than involving me!'

She could feel the muscles under her curled fingers taut and hard and she would have slid them away, broken the contact with him, if he had allowed her to. Instead he crushed her hand against him so hard that she cried out and looked up in alarm.

'You hurt me!'

'I did not hurt you, I simply squeezed your fingers—

47

I am sure you have experienced such a thing before!'

They were near the house and she hoped they weren't going to be arguing when she said goodbye to Latife. 'You didn't have to come and look for me,' she reminded him in a small quiet voice. 'If you hadn't I couldn't have—used you, or whatever it is you accuse me of.'

He said nothing, but ushered her into the house with a hand in the small of her back, and she went without protest, even though she felt angry with herself for doing so. Latife was waiting to say goodnight, holding out her hands to her as she came in, and smiling. She was only two years younger than Nuri but plump and pretty and not a bit like him.

'You look flushed, *bebek*, has Nuri been scolding you for spending so long in the gardens with your new cousin?'

Seeing him safely out of earshot and in conversation with his brother-in-law, Laurette pulled a face. 'I've been lectured by big brother on the wickedness of provoking men's jealousy.'

'That surprises you?' Laurette blinked at her uncertainly, and Latife laughed softly, squeezing her hands together between her own. 'Of course he lectured you, though I'm surprised he has been so frank about it. Perhaps—hmm?'

She was smiling and nodding and Laurette looked at her in complete mystification. 'Latife, I don't know what you're talking about; he complained that——'

'But of course he complained!' She kissed her cheek gently, her hand curved about Laurette's cheek. 'Foolish *bebek*, do you not realise that Nuri has always been jealous of whoever you talk to?' She turned to kiss her brother, leaving Laurette too stunned to answer her. 'Goodnight, little one!'

CHAPTER THREE

HALET sat curled up beside Laurette on the ottoman, her huge dark eyes shining as she watched her. 'He is calling to see you? But how exciting, Laurette! Do you think it is exciting that a young man is calling to see you?'

Knowing full well that Halet saw such an event as a prelude to serious courtship, Laurette answered cautiously. 'It will be nice to see Ian again. After all, it isn't every day that I discover relatives I didn't know I had, and we got along very well together.'

Halet nodded, as if she read between those lines easily enough. 'I am so eager to see this new cousin you have discovered—I cannot wait for him to come!'

'But you've already met him!' Laurette's smile teased her, but gently. Halet was probably much more excited about Ian's appearance than she was herself, and very definitely for a different reason. 'Or weren't you interested enough to notice him until you discovered he was my cousin?'

'Oh, but of course!' Realising that she was being teased, she shrugged, admitting it with a rueful smile. 'I noticed only a man with red hair,' she confessed. 'There were so many people there and I did not notice if he was handsome.'

'You were with Hussein,' Laurette smiled, 'so I'm surprised you noticed him at all.' Halet blushed and hastily looked down at her hands. 'Anyway, Ian isn't handsome, though he's attractive.'

'You think him very attractive?'

Laurette nodded, though it was obvious that by admitting it she was giving more scope to Halet's already fertile imagination. 'Me and quite a few other females, I would imagine—he gave me the impression he's that kind of man.'

'Ah!' It was incredible that such innocent-looking eyes could suggest so much, but Halet somehow conveyed a whole world of meaning in a brief glance. 'He is of the world, this cousin of yours, eh?'

Ian was a man of the world, Laurette supposed; or he had given her that impression on the first meeting. Perhaps it would be fairer to wait until she knew him better before passing judgment, however, in case she had been wrong.

'I honestly don't know, Halet. I think he probably is, but it's hardly fair to make a judgment on one meeting. There's no doubt that he's very confident and sure of himself.'

Halet, with her experience limited to the very self-confident men of her own immediate circle of family and friends, looked vaguely puzzled. 'But surely you would expect a man to be so, Laurette,' she remarked innocently, and Laurette smiled.

'Perhaps—though Nuri can shake his confidence to some extent. I noticed it the other night when they met.' Heaven knew why she had seen fit to comment on it, but the fact had intrigued her somehow, and she remembered it.

'Nuri does not like him?'

She made it sound less like a question than a foregone conclusion, Laurette thought, and wondered suddenly if Halet too harboured the same illusions as her elder sister regarding Nuri's attitude towards her. Oddly uneasy suddenly, though for no good reason she could think of, she got up and strolled across to the windows and looked out at the gardens, hemmed in by tall cypresses and plane trees that stirred gently against a background of blue sky—a sky that appeared strangely luminous because of the proximity of the sea below the cliffs.

She turned her face to the breeze that blew in through the windows, warm and scented by the magnolias and roses, closing her eyes for a second. It was impossible to imagine herself living anywhere else now, and yet she would soon have to do just that. Yarev had been the centre of her world for the past eight years—a restricted world, as Ian had suggested, perhaps, but a comfortable one that she was reluctant to leave.

Sensing that Halet was still watching her from her seat on the ottoman, she half turned from the window to answer her. 'I don't know whether or not Nuri likes him, but *I* do, and that's what matters as he's my cousin.'

'And will you——'

Halet stopped in mid-sentence, turning her head when the door opened. Nuri came just inside the room and stood with one hand on the handle while he noted his sister's presence with a nod that seemed to indicate satisfaction. Then swiftly his black gaze switched to Laurette and she realised the reason for that nod of satisfaction even before he spoke.

'Mr Kearn is here to see you, Laurette.'

His quiet voice somehow managed to express both disapproval and politeness, and she could see Ian standing just behind him waiting, a glimmer of amusement in his eyes. Smiling, she walked across, and Nuri stepped back to allow him into the room.

51

'Hello, Ian!'

It was a surprise, even to her, when he came straight to her and kissed her, taking her hands in his, and she distinctly heard Halet's swift indrawn breath. 'Hello, cousin!' He used the title merely to emphasise his right to kiss her, she thought, but found it hard to ignore Nuri's black-eyed gaze from the doorway.

She looked across at him and caught his eye for a second, her heart thudding unexpectedly hard when she saw something there that would seem to suggest Latife had been right about him. It was the impression of only a second before those thick black lashes came down to hide it, but briefly she saw a fierce burning glitter of raw emotion in his eyes, and caught her breath.

'If you will excuse me, I am required elsewhere!'

She smiled at him, caught unaware and not quite sure of herself. 'Oh yes, of course, Nuri—thank you.'

Ian merely nodded his thanks, smiled amiably, and murmured some polite phrase that suggested he neither knew nor cared whether he was there or not. He was nervous, she guessed, she could tell it from the clasp of his hands, but he was concealing it very well, and she was once more intrigued by the idea of him being unnerved by Nuri being there.

Scarcely had the door closed behind her brother before Halet was on her feet, standing there uncertainly for a moment and knowing full well, Laurette suspected, that Nuri would expect her to stay for as long as Ian was with her. But Halet could on occasion show some of the independence that being with Laurette had taught her, and she was ready to leave them together, regardless of what Nuri wanted.

'You've met Halet, haven't you, Ian?'

He stood holding Laurette's hand, but turned a smile

on Halet that obviously disarmed her. 'I met Miss Kayaman at the same party I met you, Laurette.' He took her hand and shook it, his hold lingering slightly longer than was necessary so that Halet blushed and glanced at Laurette hastily. 'It was a very delightful party,' he declared, his meaning unmistakable. 'How are you, Miss Kayaman?'

Halet murmured polite words in her own tongue, her English deserting her for the moment, then looked at Laurette once more. 'I too will leave you, Laurette. *Lütfen müsade edin.*'

She started towards the door, but Ian was quick to forestall her, his wide, encouraging smile in evidence again. 'Oh no, please don't let me drive you away, Miss Kayaman! Laurette and I are going out, there's no need for you to disturb yourself on my account.'

Laurette had no idea what he had in mind for them, but she nevertheless hastened to add her plea to his. 'Oh no, please don't let us drive you out, Halet.' The hand he slid under her arm felt very possessive, and yet she could not admit enough dislike of the situation to do anything about changing it. 'I don't know where we're going, but if Ian says——'

'I had thought you might like to show me the ruins of Aspendus; they're something of an attraction, I believe, aren't they?'

The blue eyes below copper-brown hair seemed to be challenging her to find fault with his plan, and at the moment she saw no reason to. It wasn't quite what she had expected him to have in mind when he said they were going out, but in a way it was a relief that his plan involved nothing more complicated than showing him the ruins of the ancient city of Aspendus.

'Aspendus is one of the well-known ones—there are quite a number in fact.'

53

'And do you know enough of the subject of archaeology to act as my guide, pretty cousin?' The question sounded serious enough, but it was clear from the look in his eyes that he realised just how he was hustling her into falling in with his plans, and she instinctively angled her chin in a way that Nuri would have recognised.

'I'm not an expert, Ian, but I think I know enough to make it interesting for you.'

'Good!' He bent his head and looked directly down into her eyes. 'I had a feeling you wouldn't let me down somehow.'

Her pulses fluttered warningly as she drew back a little and looked down at the pretty cotton lawn dress she was wearing. 'This dress will do, won't it? It's cool and comfortable.'

'And almost the same gorgeous blue as your eyes.' He gave her one of his disarming grins, then turned her about with the hand he had under her arm. 'You look good enough to eat, cousin, so be warned!'

It was quite clear that Halet found such blatant flattery breathtaking. Hussein had never put his feeling for her so boldly into words for others to hear; but then Hussein could say so much with his fine dark eyes. Laurette caught Halet's hand before Ian could bustle her out of reach, and smiled at her, understanding her reaction better than Ian ever could.

'I don't suppose I shall be very late, Halet.'

'But don't bank on it!' Both girls looked at him, and he grinned from one to the other, settling eventually on Laurette. 'There's no rush, is there? We might go on somewhere else afterwards.'

'Oh—yes, of course.' Laurette was used to having Nuri make his opinion known in no uncertain way, but that was usually in the direction of curbing her activities, not encouraging them, and she took a second to accustom herself to the change. 'Well, of course there's no need to hurry at all, although I wouldn't want to be so late that Baba Refik would start wondering if something had happened to me.'

'Or brother Nuri?'

The words were meant for her alone, and he whispered them against her ear. Her face flooding with sudden colour, she shook her head hastily. 'Ian, I wish you wouldn't——'

'Oh, come on, my sweet!' Squeezing his fingers into her arm, he drew her with him to the door. 'I'm not trying to kidnap you!'

His eyes had a bright sparkling look that in part suggested impatience, and she hastily turned to wave a hand at Halet before they left the *salon*. 'If you want to see Aspendus, then I'll give you the full tour!'

Ian dipped his head and kissed her neck lightly. 'That's my girl!'

Driving through the fertile countryside gave Laurette the opportunity to show her knowledge of the country she had come to regard more and more as her own. Ian kept their speed down to a pace that enabled him to follow her descriptions, but even so the thirty-four kilometres between Antalya and the ancient site of Aspendus was swallowed up in a surprisingly short time.

Inland slightly and driving east they ran through acre upon acre of citrus crops after they left the town behind them. Oranges, lemons and grapefruit grew prolifically in the fertile soil, and the ubiquitous olive sprawled its ghostly grey branches against the blue sky and the towering majesty of the Taurus mountain range, the impressive Toros Daglari that dominated this part of Turkey.

The lower slopes of the mountains were thick with dark pine forests that swept down from below the snow line to the curiously patterned foothills, and gave only occasional tantalising glimpses of the falls of clear water rushing down from the mountain snows.

Stone walls divided each smallholding from its neighbour, and rows of tall cypresses acted as wind-breaks as well as contributing to the beauty of the landscape. Little houses with their small portions of land, set like sections of a mosaic over the vastness of the Anatolian plain.

In no time at all, it seemed, they were turning off the main highway and on to a secondary road to Aspendus. Like most ruins of its kind, the ancient city was on a hill with a river not too far away, and its location was evident for some time before their arrival, indicated by the tall towers of its once effective aqueduct striding across the countryside from the mountains.

The town itself was mostly Roman, that much Laurette knew, and she hoped she was going to prove as effective a guide as Ian obviously expected. The theatre was the main attraction, and it was there that she took him first, making unhesitatingly for the entrance in the central façade, a fact that Ian noted and remarked on as he followed her through in to the huge auditorium.

'You *do* know your way around, don't you?'

She smiled at him over her shoulder and nodded. 'Quite well, I suppose.'

'Are you by way of being an archaeologist?'

She laughed, shaking her head. 'Heavens, no, but Nuri's quite a well-known amateur one, and he's always ready to talk about it. I've always been fairly interested.'

'Did he bring you here?'

Once more she shook her head, but this time unaccompanied by even a smile. 'Nuri comes with other archaeologists—I'd get in the way.'

'I see!' Ian was chuckling, as if the idea amused him, and she was driven to wondering if he was quite as different from Nuri as might at first appear. 'But you have been before, I gather?'

'Occasionally.'

Laurette led the way round, pointing out the many well-preserved features of the nearly two-thousand-year-old building. Ian listened, he might even have taken some of it in, but she thought he was more interested in how she had acquired what knowledge she had.

'You come alone?' he asked.

'I have been alone.' She made the admission reluctantly, as if it was not something she felt she should admit. 'But I've also been a couple of times with some American friends of Baba Refik's—they knew I was interested, and they asked me if I'd like to come along. Baba Refik was quite happy to let me go with them, he wouldn't have liked to think of me walking around here alone.'

She pointed out an inscription in Latin and Greek that gave the name of the architect as well as those of the patrons and the gods to whom the theatre had been dedicated, but Ian was more interested at the moment in the fact that it was frowned on for her to come alone. He was looking at her curiously, a gleam in his blue eyes that she did not quite understand.

'Do you mean you're not allowed out alone? Not even to look around a ruined city?'

'Well, of course I'm allowed out, Ian, it's just that he'd worry if he thought I was out here on my own.'

They were in the entrance to one of the side passages that flanked the stage on either side, and she stopped in

57

the cool shade and leaned against a wall for a moment, wondering if he would ever really understand the way things were. It was so much harder than she would have believed to get him to see things in their proper perspective, and not be annoyed at what he saw as restrictions on her freedom.

'I've told you, I have been here alone, Ian. Though I've never been when there's been anything going on—I would rather like to come then.'

Briefly distracted, Ian looked around at the huge, well preserved and restored auditorium. Divided into two by an aisle, it would have seated thousands, though scarcely in comfort, and it was spanned by a gallery of elegant arches which would have taken yet more people. It was vast and impressive but not really beautiful.

'Do you mean to tell me that this place is still used?'

Thankful to have interested him in something other than her own situation with the Kayamans, she smiled. 'Oh yes, occasionally. They hold folk music festivals here sometimes, and wrestling matches.'

The way Ian was looking at her told its own story. 'There wouldn't happen to be a festival on about now, would there?'

The idea of coming with him to see a festival was one that intrigued her, and it was plain when she shook her head that she regretted the loss of opportunity. 'You're too late, I'm afraid, Ian. There was one last month, but there's nothing now.'

He knew exactly how much she would have liked to come with him, it showed in the way he smiled, and he reached for her hands and squeezed them lightly, looking down into her eyes as he spoke. 'Nothing? Not even some Turkish gladiators wrestling each other? What a pity!'

'Oh, but there——'

She stopped hastily, foreseeing the problems it could cause if she went on and hoping he would not follow up her impulsive, half-formed sentence. Ian lifted her chin, taking note of the flush in her cheeks and the thick lashes that hid her eyes from him. His fingers stroked her skin, coaxing her to look up.

'But?' he prompted her gently, and she looked up at last. 'What *is* on in this ancient ruin, Laurette? Something so barbaric that you'd faint away at the sight of it?'

'Oh no, of course not! But—well, it's wrestling, Ian, and women don't attend wrestling matches.'

'They do, you know. They attend them all the time in England, *and* shout louder than anybody in support of their heroes!'

'I—I don't like it.'

'Have you ever seen it?' She shook her head, and he smiled. 'Well, there you are, then—how do you know you won't enjoy it? We could pass as a couple of tourists if you're squeamish about the Kayamans' reputation.'

Laurette broke his hold, eased her chin from those stroking fingers and walked off a few steps, and when she moved from the shadowed passage and into the sun, it caught her hair and turned it to flame. Her creamy skin took on a creamy gold look with dark shadows where her lashes lay on her cheeks, and to the man in the shadows she looked slightly unreal.

It was one of those moments when her two worlds came into conflict, and she felt alarmingly unable to cope for a second or two. For her part she would have been willing enough to come with Ian to watch the wrestling, but her foster-father's reaction would be another matter. Baba Refik wouldn't be angry, that would be Nuri's reaction, but he would be concerned, and Nuri would bring home his father's concern to her without hesitation. She had become one of them almost to the extent that Baba Refik actually thought of her as a daughter, and he would never have considered allowing Halct to go. Perhaps to Ian the idea was unreasonable, but it was a fact.

'Ian, it's—it's different here. It isn't that I don't want to come with you, but I know that, while he wouldn't stop me from coming, he wouldn't be happy about it either.'

'Nuri?' He said it so softly that from her place in the sun she scarcely heard him.

'I'm talking about Baba Refik, not Nuri, you know that, Ian!'

He said nothing more for a second or two while he leaned against the ancient stone with his face in the shadows, his blue eyes fixed on her with disturbing steadiness. 'You set great store by the opinion of Father Refik, don't you, Laurette?'

'I love him.' Her own statement took her somewhat by surprise, although she realised it was quite true. During the eight years that Refik Kayaman had taken her under his care, she had become as fond of him as she had been of her own father. 'He's been very good to me, and I don't like to do anything he doesn't approve of, Ian. I don't think you can understand.'

Taking a cigarette from his case, he lit it, then leaned back once more, blowing smoke from between pursed lips until it formed a hazy blue screen in front of his face. 'I understand one thing, Laurette. I understand very well that you're fast becoming far too much of a harem maiden, and less and less Angus Kearn's daughter. And I can't believe he meant that to happen.'

'No!'

Her eyes showed as much confusion as anger at the charge, and she wished she was more sure of herself.

How could both he and Nuri be right about her? Nuri thought her far too brashly outspoken more often than not, and Ian saw her as over-protected and so sheltered that she did nothing without her foster-father's approval. Something in between must surely be the truth, but she looked at him for a second or two in confusion, then turned and walked a short distance along to the centre aisle.

'I'm not restricted in any way, Ian. I can come and go as I please, but——' She raised her hands in a gesture of helplessness, then turned once more and looked at him appealingly. 'I wish you could understand, Ian. It isn't because I'm not allowed to do certain things that I don't do them, but in deference to—my host, if you like. Refik Kayaman is a good man, and he made me a part of his family, I can't act in outright defiance of his customs.'

'Not even when they're outmoded?'

She hated his sarcasm, her expression showed it. 'I know things are different for a woman in Turkey now; they have a lot more freedom to do as they like and behave as they like, but some families, quite a few you'll find, still follow the old traditions to some degree or other. They change more slowly—Baba Refik is one of those, but it would be ungrateful and bad-mannered not to comply with the reservations he still has.'

'Oh, Laurette!' Ian came to her, taking her hands and holding them tightly while they stood out there in the vast auditorium where the sun turned their two bright heads to burnished copper. 'I'm not trying to influence you against your family, but sooner or later you have to break with them and their traditions, you've said so yourself, and it isn't long now, is it?'

She shook her head, her voice small and muffled. 'Less than two months.'

'And you'll be out on your own. I'm just trying to help the process of conditioning you. To ease you out of that cosy little shell you're in, if I can.'

It wasn't at all easy to think clearly and sensibly at the moment, but she had to admit that some of what was said was true. Possibly she had become less independent during the past few years, although she thought Nuri would never have agreed with him, but Halet's marriage was going to change a great many things. This man with his red hair and his boisterous confidence was like her father in a lot of ways; he was family, her own family.

There was someone other than the Kayamans with an interest in her future now, and he had more right to his interest, he was her own flesh and blood. And yet she could not bring herself to accept him as such. He was a stranger she had met at a party and liked, but he didn't have that closeness that she felt with the Kayamans, a closeness built on shared years together as a family—not yet.

Ian raised her chin on his flat palm and she caught her breath. His smile like his voice, was more restrained than usual. 'You don't have to offend anyone, Laurette, just gradually ease away, establish your individuality, as you have to very soon anyway.'

She raised her eyes and studied him for a moment, knowing he was right, but vaguely puzzled as to why he was taking so much trouble to concern himself with the prospects of a virtual stranger. 'Why are you bothering about me so much, Ian? I know you're my cousin,' she hastened to add, 'but you scarcely know me, do you?'

The blue eyes that looked down at her were darkly serious. 'That is something I hope to do something about from now on.'

'Because——'

He bent his head and kissed her mouth, then smiled down at her with something of his former brightness. 'Because you're a very pretty girl, and because you're my cousin!' He stroked the crown of her copper-red head and grinned. 'And we're a matched pair, aren't we?'

It was not so very much further to drive on to Side after they left the ruins of Aspendus, and Laurette had not liked to deter Ian from going on. But then neither of them could have known that the car was going to break down and delay their leaving Side for more than three hours, while a mechanic did his best to speed the repair.

By the time they were once more driving back along the motorway towards Antalya it was well gone eleven o'clock, and they had been gone for more than eight hours, with another hour's driving still in front of them. Of course midnight was no late hour for a grown woman to be out on a date, but it was the length of time they had been gone that troubled her, for almost certainly Refik Kayaman and Halet would have convinced themselves she had been involved in an accident.

As they sped along the highway the orange and lemon groves had a dreamlike quality in the moonlight, and the snow caps on the mountains glistened like floss above the darkness of the pine forests. It was a beautiful landscape, even at night, and Laurette wished she was more in a mood to appreciate it. Coming into the outskirts of Antalya at last, she glanced at her watch and saw that it was almost midnight.

'Worried?'

Ian asked the question quietly, turning his head for barely a second as he drove through the tree-lined streets, and she shook her head. She checked the time yet again as he drove along the shadowed street to where Yarev, the Kayaman home, stood back from the road among its trees and shrubs, the iron gate closed and the plume-like cypress beside it casting a long dark shadow across the wall.

'You *are* worried!'

She shook her head, though with not much conviction, apparently, for when he stopped the car Ian turned in his seat and took her hands in his. 'Shall I come in with you and explain?'

'Oh no, please, you don't have to do that, Ian.'

He looked at her for a moment in the dark interior of the car, then shrugged. Getting out of his seat he came round to lend her a hand. 'I *will* come in if it'll help, Laurette.'

'There's really no need, no one will eat me.' She laughed, but it sounded far too much like a nervous giggle, and she did not understand the strange curling sensation she felt in her stomach at all. 'It's a bit like the fairy story, isn't it? It's almost exactly midnight.'

Ian put his hands on her shoulders and held her for a moment, his blue eyes dark in the moonlight. 'Well, I shan't turn into a mouse or whatever it was, I can assure you, sweetheart.'

She smiled, shaking her head. 'I'd better go in, Ian, and let them know I haven't been run over or——'

'Abducted?' he suggested softly, and laughed at her look of surprise. 'Oh, don't think Nuri won't have thought about that too!'

'That's silly!'

Ian studied her for a second, then smiled and shrugged. 'Maybe you're right.' Drawing her to him, he put his arms around her and pressed his mouth to hers in a kiss that lasted much longer than she expected and left her breathless as she pushed his arms away. He looked down at her with a raised brow and a hint of smile on his mouth. 'I was allowed a kiss, wasn't I, cousin?'

'Yes, of course. I've had a lovely time, Ian, I really have, and I'm glad I came.' She glanced through her lashes at him, her heart beating hard in her breast. 'I hope you ask me to come again.'

'Would you come?'

'Of course!'

He said nothing for a moment, then he bent his head again swiftly and kissed her mouth, lightly and gently, before he released her. 'You'd better go in and let your folks know you're all in one piece. I'll call you tomorrow, if that's O.K.'

She nodded, one hand already on the gate that barred her way, and it opened with the betraying squeak she had never realised was quite so loud before. 'Goodnight, Ian.'

Flitting like a light-coloured shadow along the path between the magnolias and roses, she felt curiously furtive and wondered at the sense of anticipation she was suddenly experiencing, that set her heart racing fast as she reached for the door handle. Baba Refik and Nuri would still be up without a doubt, it wasn't late by their standards. She rather hoped Halet would be there too, for somehow she felt very alien suddenly in the familiar surroundings, and it was not a sensation she liked.

In the hall the hanging brass lamps shed their yellow glow on mirrors and white walls, and blurred the patterns of the exquisitely woven rugs into soft, muted fusions of colour. Her footsteps clicked softly across the tiled floor and stopped at once when the door of the *salon* opened.

The light from the room spilled like an extra bright splash of yellow across the hall floor, and along its length Nuri's shadow ran like a black dart almost to her feet. He said nothing, but Laurette automatically changed course and walked over to him, breathing an inward sigh of relief when she looked and saw that his father was seated in the room behind him. There was no sign of Halet, but Refik Kayaman was reassurance enough that she would not have to face Nuri alone.

'Baba Refik!' She walked straight past Nuri, conscious of the bright glittering black eyes that followed her as she brushed against him and the tautness of his hand on the edge of the door. She sat down beside the old man on the ottoman and looked at him with big apologetic eyes. 'I'm so sorry to be back so late, but we had a mishap.'

'A mishap?' Refik Kayaman was much like his son would be in another thirty years or so, tall and dark and fiercely proud, but with a gentleness that Nuri rarely if ever allowed to show in his character. His hair was greying, but still mainly black and cut close to his head, and his features were the same hawkish, dusky gold as his son's. 'You were involved in an accident, *bebek*? Are you hurt?'

'Oh no, I'm perfectly all right—it wasn't an accident, not a real accident.'

'You said a mishap.' Nuri's voice held that sound of suppressed anger that she knew so well, and he came and sat in a chair facing her, his eyes unwavering as he fixed them on her, as if he dared her to account for her lateness without resorting to lies. 'If you have not been involved in an accident, what other reason could you have for letting your family worry about you for all these hours?'

'I'm sorry.'

'Not so sorry that you did not take yet more time to stand with Ian Kearn in the street outside before you came in!'

'Laurette!' Refik Kayaman's hands pressed hers gently and brought her back from the brink of yet another quarrel with Nuri. 'Tell me what happened, *bebek*.'

Ignoring Nuri's harsh challenging gaze, she gave her attention to his father. 'We went from Aspendus on to Side. It was silly, I suppose, to go on to anywhere else, but——' she shrugged and ventured a small apologetic smile at the man beside her, 'Ian wanted to go, and we would have been back much sooner if only the car hadn't broken down in Side.'

'Ah, the car had the mishap, hmm?' Refik Kayaman smiled at her, and patted her hand understandingly. 'I am glad that it was not you who was hurt, *bebek*, but we have been very concerned about you being gone for so long. If you had telephoned——'

'Oh, Baba Refik!'

She gazed at him in stunned realisation. The solution had been at her fingertips the whole time and she had not even thought of it. Possibly the idea might have occurred to her if she had not been so concerned with watching the mechanic and thinking that every minute he was going to tell them everything was right again and they could be on their way. It should have occurred to her, but it simply hadn't.

The sound that Nuri made with his mouth was impatience, anger, all manner of uncomplimentary opinions, and he got to his feet again, as if by doing so he could express himself more forcefully. As he towered over her, his mouth was a tight angry line in the chiselled harshness of his face.

'It did not even occur to you to telephone? Are you so foolish, Laurette, that you did not realise we would be concerned when you were gone so long with a strange man for company?'

'Ian *isn't* a stranger, he's my cousin!'

67

'You have seen him only once before, you little fool! Do you trust yourself to every stranger you meet in the same way? Because he tells you he is your cousin——'

'He *is* my cousin!'

She wished she did not feel so small sitting there while he towered above her like some gigantic Nemesis. He had no right to speak to her the way he was, and she would let him know it. Getting to her feet, she stood in front of him, her red hair shining like burnished copper in the lamplight, and her blue eyes blazing.

'And you have a lot less right to yell at me than he has! I won't be treated like a—runaway schoolgirl every time I go on a date with Ian! I have a right to go with whom I please and for as long as I please!'

'Even though we wait to hear that you have been hurt or worse because you have been so long?'

'I'm *sorry*!' She rolled her hands tightly, breathing hard and fast as if she had run a very long way. 'I wouldn't have deliberately done anything to worry Baba Refik and he knows that—he isn't yelling at me! I'm not your sister, Nuri, and you don't have the right to bully me the way you do Halet!'

'You little——'

'Nuri!'

His father's voice recalled him, speaking quietly in his own tongue, and he stood for a moment almost trembling with anger, his black eyes more blazingly furious than Laurette had ever seen them. Facing him aroused a curious kind of reaction in her that was neither fear nor excitement, but a confusing mixture of both. She did not remember ever holding his gaze so firmly before, but she did so now for a full half minute before he turned swiftly and went striding across the room and out of the door.

His tread rang firmly on the tiled hall floor before it

was deadened by the carpeted stair treads a few moments later, and Laurette stood with her hands rolled tightly as she listened to it, her eyes wide and unbelieving. When she let out her breath it came in a long sigh and left her body trembling so that she sank down on to the ottoman again beside her foster-father.

Viewed in the cool light of reason, she supposed, she had no cause to feel as she did. Nuri had lost his temper and berated her and she had retaliated, but now, as always, she was regretting having quarrelled with him. Perhaps more than usual, for she could still see that blazing fury in his eyes, and shiver.

'Oh, Baba Refik, what have I done?'

The old man reached for her hand and gently held it in his for a moment. 'You have offended Nuri's pride, and he is very angry at the moment, child, but he will forgive you.'

He sounded so confident and she wanted to believe it, but it was too hard to forget the look in Nuri's eyes when he strode from the room. 'He might not. I—I think I've really upset him this time, and I really don't mean to.' She looked at him anxiously, her eyes seeking reassurance in the face that so much resembled Nuri's, yet showed so much more understanding and compassion. 'Baba Refik, if I say I'm sorry I spoke as I did, and——'

'You both spoke in anger, *bebek*. In the morning you will both be more calm and you will both say that you are sorry—it will all be over, hmm?'

'Nuri won't, I know him!'

Refik Kayaman squeezed her hand and smiled, his dark eyes filled with gentle laughter. 'And I too know him, little one—trust me to know him better, eh?'

CHAPTER FOUR

It was not going to be nearly so easy making it up with Nuri this time, Laurette realised, not after last night's incident, and the thought troubled her intensely. Usually their quarrels were ended by mutual consent and with very little being said. A murmured apology, and Nuri would regard her for a second or two before showing that hint of a smile that sometimes softened his straight firm mouth, and it was all over.

Somehow in her heart she felt it was going to be different this time. She had a premonition that things had changed in a way she could not yet define, and she approached the idea of facing him with much more caution than usual.

At present Nuri was alone in the *salon*, she knew. He always took time to go through the morning papers before he started the business of the day, and he would be in there now, doing just that. But at any moment the closed door was likely to open and he would come striding out, on his way to the offices in Antalya, and the opportunity would be lost to her.

Halet was upstairs, and Refik Kayaman about some business of his own, so that she would never have a better opportunity. She was no more than half way across the hall when the door of the *salon* opened and, just as she anticipated, Nuri came striding out. Catching sight of her, he paused and would probably have spoken, but she feared he might instead go off without saying anything, and she called out to him.

'Nuri!'

His black eyes watched her as she hurried across to him, and she felt again that disturbing sense of uncertainty, that things were not as usual. She would have spoken then, asked him to give her a few minutes before he left, but he stepped back and pushed open the door of the *salon* again, indicating that she should go in.

Walking past him, she felt much the same as she had when she came home last night, for he held the door open as he had then, and his black-eyed gaze followed her in the same way, except that their expression was more carefully guarded this morning by thick dark lashes.

It was by instinct that she made for the big comfortable ottoman on the far side of the room, and sat on it with one foot curled up under her and the other on the floor. The fat cushions plumped up around her so that she looked smaller even than she actually was, and with Nuri standing, as he had last night, she felt curiously anxious.

She had anticipated it being harder than usual after last night, but she was dismayed to realise just how difficult it was. She had never felt so distant from him before, and she disliked the sensation far more than she cared to admit. With her body held unconsciously stiff and straight and her head down, from where he stood Nuri could see only the crown of her copper-red head and the vulnerable curve of her neck as she sat with a hand either side of her, flat-palmed on the cushions, not looking at him.

'Please—won't you sit down too, Nuri? I—I feel rather as if you're towering over me while you're standing there.'

Rather surprisingly, he made no demur about it, but

dropped down beside her on the ottoman instead of using one of the chairs as she hoped. 'You wish to—talk, hmm?'

It was not an easy opening, for it threw the onus on to her, and she was much too unsure of herself at the moment to know quite how to begin. 'Nuri, last night——'

'Last night you were angry.'

'So were you!'

She looked up quickly, her bottom lip caught between her teeth, then as hastily looked down again. The retort had been impulsive but unfortunate, and she waited to see whether or not he was ready to accept that he too had been at fault. Somewhat unexpectedly, he did.

'We were both angry, we will agree on that, Laurette, if on nothing else.'

The quiet way he spoke was unexpected too in a way, and she looked at him briefly again, trying to determine his mood, but those concealing lashes still hid his expression from her. She could not even guess whether he was actually as cool and calm as he appeared to be.

'You wish me to apologise for my part in that—scene, last night?' Without waiting for confirmation, he went on, 'Very well, Laurette. I will admit that I was wrong to call you a fool; I am sorry about that.'

It seemed he was going to say more, but thought better of it, and she was ready enough to do her part to heal the breach now that he had made the first move. Her pulses were fluttering, disturbed by something she could not yet recognise, and she looked up at him, anxious to have it over and done with.

'And I'm sorry I accused you of bullying Halet.'

A glimmer of a smile flitted across his dark face for a second and she took heart from it. 'By your standards I probably do bully Halet, but she would not think of my concern in the same light as you do, Laurette. That is the difference between you.'

The admission, even with the qualification he made, was unexpected, and she viewed his attitude with even more uncertainty while he leaned back on the cushions and crossed his long legs one over the other, his eyes regarding her steadily.

'Then—then if we both forget everything the other said last night, the whole episode is closed, and——'

She did not go on because something in his eyes gave her cause to doubt what she was saying suddenly. 'Not everything, Laurette. I have apologised for calling you a fool, because I do not believe it is true; in that I was wrong. But I cannot change my view that you were thoughtless in the way you behaved. It is plain, however, that you could not be expected to come home alone by public transport, and since you were not driving yourself you could do little about going on to Side.'

'So you're blaming Ian for the whole thing!' There was colour in her cheeks and the danger sign of an increased urgency in her heart beat. They were on the brink of another quarrel, and she drew back hastily from the prospect, shaking her head and avoiding looking at him once more. 'I wish you wouldn't blame Ian, Nuri, it was as much my fault as his!'

'You defend him!' Even without looking at him she was aware that the black eyes were searching her face with an explicitness that was infinitely disturbing and he was shaking his head as if he found her attitude inexplicable. 'Does he mean so much to you already, this man, that you are determined to defend him so fiercely?'

Her hands were half buried in the fat cushions either side of her and curled up tightly. 'I *have* to defend him

73

against you! You seem to have developed an—an irrational dislike of Ian for some reason I can't begin to understand!'

'You think it irrational?'

It was clear from the way he repeated the accusation that he disliked it, and already Laurette saw her plans for making peace evaporating in the inevitable argument. Faced as she was with his determined and implacable dislike of Ian, how could they succeed? Hands clasped tightly together in her lap, she raised anxious eyes once more.

'I can't see any reason for it,' she confessed. 'And you *don't* like him, do you, Nuri?'

'I would say rather that I do not trust him in proximity to you,' Nuri said quietly.

'But why not?' The look in his eyes was sufficient answer, and she shook her head hastily. 'I'm quite able to take care of myself, Nuri, and Ian isn't the monster you seem to think he is—I promise you he isn't.'

'Would you know, Laurette?' He asked the question soft-voiced but gave her no time to reply. 'He is—attracted to you?' His big hands made much more of the simple question, and she flushed. 'Of course he is, otherwise he would not trouble himself with you.'

'But he's my cousin! Naturally he'd want to see me again!'

His smile made her curiously uneasy, and vaguely angry too, but he was glancing at his watch and he got to his feet, as if he had no more time to spend on discussing her relationship with Ian. 'I have to meet some friends very shortly, I must go.'

'Having tried to make me suspect Ian of—heaven knows what?'

She could have left it there, she told herself, but something, as always, drove her on, and the look she sent him from the shadow of her thick lashes was challenging as well as defensive. Looking down at her, Nuri's eyes narrowed, a warning sign she should have heeded.

'Consider for a moment if you were plain and unattractive, Laurette. Do you seriously think that Ian Kearn is the kind of man who would concern himself with your welfare in those circumstances?'

He was convinced that Ian was an opportunist in search of a casual affair, cousin or not, and she despaired of ever making him see any differently, but she got to her feet, rather than just sit there, and stood facing him, though with no idea of what she wanted to say.

'Nuri, I know you don't like him, and you don't trust him, but he is—well, he's my family really, and when I have to leave here, when Halet marries and I'm —cut off——'

The hand that suddenly curved about her cheek and persuaded her to raise her head was unexpected, and the strong fingers had a curiously caressing touch that brought an urgent thudding beat to her heart. 'But you will not be cut off, Laurette. I cannot think what has given you such an idea.'

She lifted her eyes only as far as his mouth. The strong straight line of it was softened by something that was not quite a smile, but was infinitely gentle and reassuring. 'You said I couldn't stay on here with just you and Baba Refik, and I have to find somewhere of my own. Ian can help me, I might even go to——'

'You do not need his help!' His mouth looked harder again now and less gentle than adamant; the fingers on her cheek holding her more tightly. 'We will always be here to help you, Laurette, if you will only trust us as you have until now.'

'Oh, but of course I trust you, only——'

'Then let me hear no more of this plan to go off with Ian Kearn, eh, *bebek*?'

It was a new situation, one she had not foreseen, and to feel so unsure of what to say or do was disturbing, especially with Nuri's black eyes looking down at her so intently. Her flesh tingled from the touch of his hand on her cheek, and she wished she had the nerve to look up at him directly—it seemed so much harder to do than it ever had before.

His fingers eased their hold and once more became a caress, his thumb moving slowly over her soft skin in a way that aroused sensations that were new to her. 'My father would miss you so much, *bebek*; would you break his heart by going right away with this man who is a stranger to you?'

From his mouth to the shadowed black eyes was a mere flicker of movement that raised her own long lashes, and her voice was shiveringly unsteady and barely above a whisper. 'I know Baba Refik would miss me, Nuri, but you——'

He said something in his own tongue, so softly she barely heard it, reaching out his arms for her and drawing her close while he was still speaking, and she felt strangely alarmed for a second before her senses responded more urgently to him. One hand tightly twined in her copper-red hair to pull back her head, he covered her mouth with his with a fierce, hard urgency that took her breath away and aroused a soft cry from her in the second before she lifted her arms around put them around his neck.

Her senses responded with an urgency that would have startled her, had she been conscious of it, and she pressed as close to the strong vigorous force of him as she could, her hands at either side of his dark head, stroking lightly with her finger-tips in the thick black hair. Her complete unawareness of anything but the need to respond to his kiss made his sudden distraction all the more startling.

He was cursing softly in his own tongue, and he turned swiftly, his arms dropping to his sides with the strong hands tightly clenched as if in anger. The look in Halet's eyes as she stood just inside the room was explanation enough—she looked almost fearful for a second, her hands to her face as she whispered something in Turkish which made Nuri turn again and look down at Laurette with his black eyes narrowed.

'Show Laurette's visitor in, Halet—I am just leaving!'

'Nuri!'

Her cry went unheeded as he strode across to the door, but he turned briefly in the doorway and glanced back at her. She had expected to see anger and the expression she saw instead took her by surprise, for it was a kind of appeal and she found it irresistible. Then he was gone; turned swiftly and striding across the hall, giving Ian only a cool, brief '*gün aydin*' as he passed him.

Normally Halet's instinct would have led her to leave at once, but instead she hesitated and her dark eyes, wide and anxious, regarded Laurette's flushed face as if she expected her to be annoyed. 'Oh, Laurette, what can I say? I did not know, I am so——'

'Oh no, *please* Halet, don't apologise!' Her own voice, like Halet's was barely more than a whisper, and she laughed a little unsteadily when she heard the outside door close firmly behind Nuri. 'I don't know what came over Nuri, but by now he's probably wishing he hadn't been so impulsive!' She looked at Ian as he came across the room to her and smiled, her voice perhaps more forcedly cheerful than she realised. 'Hello, Ian, you're quite an early bird this morning.'

He sensed something in the air, that was obvious, and his eyes switched from her to Halet and back again, plainly curious. 'Am I *too* early? I thought perhaps after last night—I felt rather bad about leaving you to do all the explanations, so I came fairly early this morning in case there was anything I could clear up.'

Laurette was still trying to steady her hands and even her voice still had a betraying quiver that she did her best to disguise, though she knew Halet was still watching her and was quite frankly curious. 'Oh, there's nothing to worry about last night, Ian, that's all over and done with.'

'I see.'

She wondered just how much he could have seen from the hall when Halet first opened the door of the *salon*. Whether or not he had seen Nuri kissing her, or if his view had been obscured. If he had seen it seemed not to have deterred him, for after smiling at Halet with one of his disarming smiles, he bent and kissed Laurette's mouth, an easy arm about her shoulders.

'Are you ready to come out with me, cousin? Or do I get my marching orders after yesterday?'

It was a direct challenge, and she met it with slightly less defiance than she would have done normally, because she was still remembering the feel of Nuri's arms around her, and the hard urgent pressure of his mouth on hers. It was quite unconscious when her left hand strayed to her lips and lingered for a moment, before she hastily snatched herself back to a level of normality.

'No, of course you don't get your marching orders, Ian. But if you'll just give me a moment to see Baba Refik and let him know I'll be out for a while.'

'Sure!' It was clear from the way he said it that he

suspected her real reason was to ask permission of her foster-father, and his next words confirmed it. 'Do you have to ask his permission, Laurette?'

'No!' She answered with more vehemence than she realised, and heard Halet catch her breath. Recovering hastily, she shook her head at Ian and smiled. 'You know that isn't necessary, Ian, I told you yesterday—I'm not under restraint.'

'Sorry!'

It was difficult to be annoyed when he looked so wryly at her, and she shook her head in despair as she turned to leave. 'I won't be more than a few seconds—wait for me, won't you?'

He winked one eye, a gesture that Halet viewed with some doubt, and grinned at her amiably. 'You bet!' he said.

When they once more turned off on to the road to Aspendus there was already a little niggle of suspicion at the back of Laurette's mind, and she glanced uneasily at Ian's blandly confident face. 'Ian, if you're thinking of——'

'Surprise, my lovely!' He flashed her a smile over his shoulder, and winked an eye. 'You and I are going to be just a couple of tourists this morning, and you'll get your wish to see something actually happening in this ancient pile at last!'

'But, Ian, it's wrestling, and you know I——'

'I know that if you behave as if Nuri Bey can have you confined to the harem for the rest of your life as a punishment for behaving like a redheaded beauty should, I shall lose my temper and hit somebody!'

His voice sounded scratchily impatient, and she was too taken aback for a second or two to know what to say. To someone unaccustomed to the manners and customs of the country he was visiting, her reticence about offending her foster-father must seem annoying, but she could not do other than regard Refik Kayaman's feelings as important, no matter what Ian thought about it.

When he turned and spoke to her again he had apparently cooled down to some extent and he grinned at her ruefully. 'Sorry, love, but if you're going to become westernised you'll have to get used to making your own decisions, and behaving as if you have every right to go just anywhere you like.'

Refik Kayaman, she knew, would not have barred her from coming to the wrestling with Ian, but he would have preferred her not to go, and she did not look forward to telling him she had been. Keeping quiet about it did not even enter her head, although that was probably what Ian had in mind for her to do. Nuri's possible reaction was what concerned her most, however, and realising it both puzzled and disturbed her.

With Ian's hand on her arm she had little option but to accompany him into the huge auditorium that yesterday had been deserted except for the two of them, and today was noisy and colourful. The front seats were filled with rows of people who all seemed to be talking at once. Turkish men for the most part, sitting apart or in little groups, slightly wary of parties of mixed male and female tourists, though readily hospitable in the matter of information or assistance.

For some curious reason, Laurette had never felt more alien in the vast theatre than she did among people who spoke her own language, and her heart was thudding hard as she allowed Ian to help her to a seat just off the central aisle. From behind dark glasses, she looked about her cautiously. The Kayamans had many friends, quite a few of whom knew her, and some of them must surely be followers of wrestling.

She had almost convinced herself that there was no one there who could recognise her, when she spotted a vaguely familiar face below them in the crowd nearer the stage. The man was an acquaintance of Nuri's and, as she watched him surreptitiously from behind her dark lenses, he turned his head, almost as if the intensity of her own gaze had drawn his attention.

Her red head was never easy to miss, and when Ian was beside her they stood out like fiery beacons among the crowd. She saw the man hesitate, a frown between his brows, then he leaned across to speak to his neighbour, and she realised who was seated next to him. Hand to her face, she closed her eyes in resignation.

'Oh no!' She whispered the words, and Ian turned swiftly, his hand reaching for hers, puzzled for a moment, and she dared not look to see if Nuri had actually turned to see her for himself. 'Nuri's here! Ian, he's here, and the man with him has spotted me, he knows me!'

'Then sit tight and send him a happy smile!' Ian's eyes gleamed in a way that suggested Nuri's dislike of him was reciprocated with interest, and his hand squeezed her tightly. 'Damn it, Laurette, you have a right to be here with me!'

'Yes, I know.'

She chanced a hasty look after a moment or two, but if Nuri had ever been moved enough to turn and look at her, he was now facing firmly forward, and she sat with her hands in her lap, watching the back of his head with a kind of excitement stirring in her breast that made no sort of sense at all in view of the reaction she could expect from him later.

She looked hastily at her watch some time later when

Ian suggested they should leave, and was surprised to find how much time had passed. She had been so pre-occupied for the most part that the wrestling bouts they had come to see had gone largely unnoticed, and Ian was looking into her face with a resigned smile.

'This wasn't such a good idea, after all, was it, Laurette?'

'I'm sorry, Ian.' She wished she could sound more enthusiastic, but even now she glanced, almost unconsciously, at the dark, proud and carefully averted head down there in the crowd. 'I just wish I wasn't so sure that Nuri hates the idea of me being here. I know I shouldn't care, but I do.'

'Were you fighting when I arrived this morning?' She glanced at him, vaguely suspicious that he might know the truth, but he went on and she thought he could not have known what had actually been happening between her and Nuri. 'I don't know, but I got the impression that I'd interrupted something; you looked very flushed and shiny-eyed as if you might have been battling with Nuri Bey over something.'

Her heart was racing, thudding like a drum beat at her ribs, and she felt strangely breathless, simply remembering Nuri's kiss. Heaven knew what had possessed him in those few moments, but it was something she had never experienced before and she was almost reluctant to admit, even to herself, that she had found it incredibly exciting being kissed by him.

'We—we *had* been arguing.' She decided on a half-truth. 'About last night.'

'Ah, I thought it might have been that! He didn't stop to have it out with me, though, did he?'

'Because I didn't want him to, Ian, he knew that. You and Nuri quarrelling is the last thing I want.'

His raised brows suggested surprise and blue eyes

regarded her for a moment steadily. 'And is he in the habit of doing what you want him to?'

'No, of course not. But neither does he automatically oppose everything I do, Ian. We get along fairly well most of the time.'

'Just as long as you do as you're told, hmm?'

'No, Ian!'

'All right, all right!' They were seated by the aisle and he got to his feet, holding out a hand. 'Let's move on, shall we? I'm finding that disapproving back view down there too much of a distraction too.' He smiled at her ruefully when she looked at him, and shook his head. 'I *have* noticed you watching him, Laurette. He bothers you, whether I like it or not!'

Holding her hand tightly, he led the way outside again, then turned her to face him, looking at her for a moment with a curiously searching look in his eyes. 'It's going to come to a head soon, isn't it, Laurette? This business with Nuri Kayaman,' he went on before she had a chance to speak. 'It has to be settled one way or the other soon. He doesn't like me, that's easy to work out, and he'd stop you seeing me again if he could. The question is, are you going to let him?'

She was not even sure of the answer herself, but she said what he wanted her to say more by instinct than deliberation. 'No, Ian.'

'Good for you! Because I'm damned if I'm going to sit back and let him cut you off from contact with your own family the way he wants to!'

'Oh no, Ian, that's not true!' Denying it automatically as she did, she realised a moment later, did not make it any less possible that he was right. 'I—I have to leave Yarev when Halet marries Hussein in a little more than six weeks' time, but Nuri says——'

'Nuri says!' He cut her short abruptly, and his impatience startled her for a moment. 'I suppose he has a husband all lined up for *you* as well!'

'No, he hasn't, Ian. He knows my feelings in that matter.'

'Good God!' He was blinking as if he did not quite believe her. 'Do you mean he's actually mentioned it? They really intend to marry you off?'

'No, of course they don't, if by they you mean Baba Refik and Nuri. None of the girls have had their husbands chosen for them, they're all very much in love. You've seen Halet with Hussein— does it strike you that she's marrying him for any other reason than that she loves him?'

Ian refused to comment, but stuck to the one thing he could be sure of, because she had mentioned it herself. 'But he has had ideas about you in that direction? Obviously the question's been raised, Laurette, if you let him know how you felt about being married off!'

She looked down at their hands held tightly together, unwilling to make an issue of something that had been purely between herself and Nuri. 'Why do we have to talk about it, Ian? Can't we——'

'Because I'm not having you put up for auction, or whatever it is they do!'

'*They*, Ian, you keep saying *they*!' She looked up at him with her eyes bright and resentful. 'You talk about my family as if they were a pack of savages! I may have been born into your family, I might have your family's blood in my veins, but the Kayamans are my family now and I won't have you talk about them as if they were nothing short of barbarians!'

'Laurette!' She had stunned him, it was plain, and he held her hands so tightly she thought he did not realise just how tightly, his eyes searching her face for the

84

meek little cousin he expected. 'I put my foot right in it, didn't I?'

That smile, when it appeared, was as irresistible as ever, and she felt suddenly ashamed for having turned on him so fiercely, though she would do so again in defence of the Kayamans. Shaking her head, she smiled ruefully.

'Now you know why Nuri finds me too much for him sometimes! I blow up in his face when he doesn't expect it.'

'Poor chap!'

'Which is possibly why he suggested that I should move in and live with one of the girls until I married! Without Halet there to take the brunt, he'd probably find me too much of a handful even for him!'

It seemed more imperative than ever that he should understand the reason for that protective attitude of Baba Refik's and Nuri's, and she tried one more time to explain. He would probably get angry, but it would clear the air if she could make him understand them a little better, though she had not had much success with previous attempts.

'I wish you could see it from their point of view, Ian—Baba Refik and Nuri, I mean.' She spoke slowly, looking down at their clasped hands rather than at his face. 'The Turkish male is so instinctively protective about his womenfolk in a way you couldn't possibly understand.'

'And you count as womenfolk, do you?'

'Well, of course I do!' She sought for other words, other explanations. 'Nuri isn't browbeating me, or being unreasonable, not by Turkish standards—the old standards. He acts the way he does because he thinks you have what Daddy would have called—designs on me!'

85

'Well, he's right about that, anyway.' Ian said it quietly and his hands squeezed hers lightly while he looked deep into her eyes. 'I know I haven't known you for very long, Laurette, but there's a very good chance I shall fall in love with you, and I resent—yes, *resent* that black-eyed devil trying to cut me out of your life, no matter what his reasons are!'

'Ian——'

He bent his head and kissed her mouth, stemming the words she had no time to form. 'Don't let him do it, Laurette! Let's go out somewhere every day; let him know we mean business, and that he can't keep you under protective custody for the rest of your life!'

It was rather like being swept along by a tidal wave, and Laurette was not at all sure whether she was finding the experience exciting or alarming, or both. She enjoyed being with Ian, but she had known him for only three days, slightly less in fact, and she could not quite believe that statement about his beginning to fall in love with her, it was much too soon for him to be thinking along those lines. Also she had a great deal to lose if she allowed him to cut her off completely from her foster-family by deliberately setting out to oppose their views.

At the same time it was difficult for her to resist him when he constantly reminded her of her father. His blue eyes were bright and clear, just as she remembered her father's being, and his red head too was held at that same to-hell-with-it-all angle. It was his likeness to her father that was a large part of his fascination, she had to admit, but also he was attractive in his own right, and she liked him. He was family, and he could surely be trusted to have her best interests at heart— Nuri was too suspicious, or else he worried too much.

She was jolted out of her reverie suddenly when Ian

tugged at her hand. 'Suppose we start now by taking a boat trip?' he suggested as they made their way back to where the car was parked. 'I think I've seen motor launches for hire in Antalya, haven't I? Why don't we take one out for a while and I can introduce you to the thrill of a fast boat, scudding across the water in the sunshine? It's a wonderful experience, Laurette, you'll love it.'

'Oh, I do!'

She got a brief moment of pleasure from his look of surprise, and she was smiling when he looked down at her, vaguely suspicious, she thought. 'You do? Do you mean to tell me you've been allowed out in a motor launch—how come?'

'I've driven one myself!'

'I'm staggered!' He looked at her for a second with a strange mixture of expressions in his blue eyes, almost as if he did not quite believe her. 'How and when was that, Laurette?'

'Oh, Nuri has a launch.' Her casual reply was deliberate, though she did not stop to consider why she enjoyed surprising him so much. 'He taught me how to steer it and he occasionally lets me take the wheel, though only when he's there with me.'

'Good grief!'

She was smiling, shaking her head over his reaction. 'You see you don't know him nearly as well as you think you do, Ian. He's quite human on occasion; no,' she hastily amended the hint of sarcasm, 'he's very human and very good to me, as all his family are.'

'So you never tire of telling me.' He opened the door of the car and saw her in, then stood for a moment looking down at her. 'Just the same, will you come with me? Or don't I count as being as trustworthy as Nuri Bey?'

'Oh, Ian, of course you do!'

In fact she was curiously uncertain whether she wanted to go out in a boat with him or not, but she was not prepared to let him know it at the moment. Agreeing with him was exactly what he wanted, and he leaned over and pressed his mouth to hers, lightly at first, and then more ardently until she felt her heart begin a hard, protesting beat and tried to turn her head away.

With startling clarity she had suddenly recalled the way Nuri had kissed her, just before she came out with Ian, and again merely remembering brought on a sense of breathtaking excitement that made her much less willing to respond to Ian's kiss.

'Let's go, hmm?' Laurette nodded silently, pre-occupied once more, and he got in beside her then leaned across his seat, smiling, to lightly kiss her mouth. 'I'll show you how to get Nuri Kayaman out of your hair, my lovely, just you see!'

CHAPTER FIVE

IT was clear when they set out from Antalya that Ian would have preferred to be in sole charge of the boat they took, instead of hiring one with its own skipper. Hiring a manned motor launch had been Laurette's choice, for one thing Ian did not know the waters around Antalya as she did herself, and for another because she wanted there to be no chance of another occurrence like the last time she went out in a boat. With someone who knew both the boat and the waters, there was much less chance of their being capsized.

She said nothing to Ian about her reasons, but was insistent, and he at last yielded to her insistence, although he frowned over it as they left Antalya's tiny, picturesque harbour, tucked away below the old town. He seemed more irritable altogether, in fact, but she simply put it down to disappointment. Ian was not used to being thwarted, she guessed.

Antalya seen from the water was a familiar sight to Laurette, but one of which she never tired, and she pointed out the various places of interest as they followed the curve of the coastline, starting with Antalya itself. The old town that seemed to hover above its little harbour, and the falls of water that tumbled down from the high cliffs into the turquoise blue sea like shattered rainbows.

The sun on the water was dazzling, and they were glad of dark glasses, even though it was necessary to remove them to really appreciate the wonderful colours —pink cliffs, blue sea and a white-sanded beach that stretched, almost without break, from the beautiful bathing beach at Lara to Alanya, more than a hundred kilometres further east.

'Isn't it lovely?' She sought his approval with as much eagerness as if she was showing off her homeland, and Ian smiled, a little wryly, she thought.

'Very impressive. Those waterfalls back there, I presume they come down from the mountains? The Taurus mountains, you called them, didn't you?'

'That's right.' She hoped he was more interested than he sounded. 'Just as those delicious little streams do that pop up all over the place in Antalya itself. Only the Turks would think of letting them surface naturally and then build gardens round them!'

'Instead of harnessing the power they could provide.' His tone made it clear that he did not altogether like her very pro-Turkish attitude, and she looked at him regretfully.

'Oh, but it's very beautiful, Ian, and that's very important too.'

She noticed the way he put a hand to his forehead, a gesture he had made several times during their trip. 'Oh, don't take any notice of me, love, I'm a strictly practical Scot!'

'But surely you still like beautiful things?'

Her response was almost a plea, for her father too had been a very practical man, but he had also had a very strong appreciation of natural beauty, indeed it had been his influence that had formed her own appreciative faculties. She did not like to think of Ian falling short in that direction.

His smile suggested it was achieved with effort rather than spontaneous, and the way his eyes crinkled behind the dark glasses it appeared he was squinting against the sun despite the shading lenses. 'Oh, certainly I do, but mostly I like my beauty on two slim and lovely legs!'

'Ian!'

She glanced at the broad stocky figure of the boatman at the wheel, but supposed he was accustomed to the unconventional behaviour of the tourist in his business. He might not even have understood what was said with his limited knowledge of English as he took the boat around the coast, following the curving line of the land.

Inland the panorama had a misty, dreamlike look of soft colours, mostly various shades of green, against the background of summer blue sky and the snow-tipped Toros Dagli that dominated the landscape from the sea, just as it did on the road to Aspendus and Side. Laurette, as she watched it, could not imagine herself living anywhere else, and a sudden urgency in her heart beat made her realise just how anxious she was for her situation not to change, Ian or not.

'Aren't you glad I insisted on having someone take the wheel?' She smiled at him as they sat side by side at the rail, and Ian smiled, a curiously vague smile that puzzled her for a second.

'Oh, sure,' he said. 'Why would I want to be alone with a lovely girl?' He laughed, and she looked at him swiftly, sensing something wrong, but not sure what it was at the moment. 'What's wrong, Laurette? Are you afraid I might shock your boatman?'

He looked much more flushed than he should have done, no matter how hot it was, and there were beads of perspiration across his forehead and along his upper lip which he impatiently brushed away. Impulsively she reached up and placed a hand on his brow. His skin felt oddly chilled and at the same time stickily hot, and she frowned at him anxiously.

'Ian, are you all right?'

The man at the wheel, she thought, glanced briefly over his shoulder at them, and Ian was laughing unsteadily, with his hand again on his forehead. 'Oh yes, I think so, love. My head aches a bit, too much sun probably, but I'm O.K.'

'Maybe you should get under cover for a while. You're not used to the sun, and you've been out in it rather a lot the past couple of days.'

It was probably sound advice, but Ian was not at all willing to follow it, and she viewed his irritation more anxiously now, seeing it as part of something more than mere disappointment. 'For heaven's sake, Laurette, I'm not sickening for the dreaded tropical fever! Don't fuss, love, please—I can't stand fussy women!'

'I was thinking more of sunstroke than fever! And I'm not fussing, Ian, I'm just being practical! Red-haired people are known to be more susceptible to sunstroke.'

Removing the drops of moisture from his forehead with an impatient hand, he looked at her own copper-bright head. 'Then why aren't you affected too?'

'Because I'm used to it, I've spent most of my life in this kind of a climate. Now will you please do as I ask, Ian, and get under the awning out of the sun?'

He was not easy to convince, and it crossed Laurette's mind as she sought to persuade him that Nuri would have seen his stubbornness as a Kearn family trait, for he had accused her of the same thing many times in the past. Her appeals, however, eventually persuaded Ian to do as she suggested, and she saw him seated under the limited shade provided by a striped awning, but once having surrendered, he seemed to give in and his limpness made her so anxious that she turned and appealed to the man at the wheel.

'I think we'd better turn back; my cousin is ill.'

'*Güneş çarpması.*' The opinion was volunteered unhesitatingly, though it was little consolation to have her diagnosis confirmed so promptly and with such authority. 'The *bey* has had too much of the sun, *hanim*, he should see a *doktor* at once!'

'Then we must get back to Antalya.' She felt a dismaying sense of helplessness, and was briefly startled to find herself wishing that Nuri was there to help. 'That will be the quickest thing, won't it?'

The man was shaking his head. The boat was already heading for the shore, she noticed, and felt a flutter of uncertainty. 'This is the village of Tatlisu, *hanim*, and I know that here is a very good *doktor*.'

'There is?' She looked at the cluster of squat little houses sprawled across the background of a tiny incurved section of beach, and wondered if she ought to insist. 'You're sure there's a doctor here?'

A smile sat briefly on the wrinkled brown face, like a row of yellow-white fangs, and he nodded confidently. 'Oh, *evet, hanim*, he is my nephew!'

It seemed unlikely that a village too small to even appear on the map could provide the best medical attention, but any doctor was better than none in her present predicament, and she could hardly tell the man that she did not trust his nephew. Ian was taking very little interest in anything at the moment, but leaned back against the cockpit with his eyes closed. His forehead was damp and sticky and she was worried about him.

When he opened his eyes and looked at her it seemed as if he had difficulty in focusing. 'It's all right, Ian, we're getting you to a doctor.'

93

'Oh, for God's sake, I'm not ill!' His voice had a rasping harshness, but he fell back with a groan when he attempted to sit upright, his hands clutching his head. 'Maybe you're right, love.' He gave her a sickly smile, then hastily closed his eyes again. 'Crikey, I feel awful!'

'Just sit still.' She dabbed his forehead with her handkerchief and wished she had something cool to bathe it with. Voices reached her, flat and barely distinguishable on the warm air, and she glanced over her shoulder as the boat was steered closer inshore. 'We're putting in to a little village called Tatlisu. It's very small, but the boatman says they have a doctor here.'

'Then what?' Ian asked, his eyes still closed. 'Do I get abandoned to the mercies of the locals?'

Laurette hesitated, not yet even sure herself what was to follow his seeing the doctor. At the moment the only solution she could think of was to get help from home. There seemed no other way of transporting a sick man from the village back to Antalya.

'Then I find the nearest telephone and get someone to come and fetch us.'

In normal circumstances she felt sure he would have grasped the significance of what she said in a matter of seconds, but his reactions were much slower at the moment and it took him a while to see what it implied. 'Oh no!' He struggled up despite a throbbing head, and frowned at her stubbornly. 'I'm damned if you do, Laurette! I'm not having Nuri Kayaman coming out to rescue me like some blessed maiden in distress!' He clutched his aching head and groaned, sinking back once again, his eyes closed. 'Oh, God, I feel awful!'

'Poor Ian!' She brushed back the thick red hair from his brow and shook her head. 'There isn't much choice but to get someone to come and fetch us in the car, Ian.

You're in no state to go clambering on and off boats, you'll be much better off in a car.'

'Not Nuri Bey's car, I won't!' She sensed the boat-man turn his head as he brought the launch closer to the small stone jetty that extended from the white-sanded beach out into deeper water. 'No, Laurette, I won't let you—I won't be——'

'Ian, be sensible! I can't manage on my own—you're ill and I can't cope with you alone, I need someone to help.'

'All right, all right!' He put both hands to his head when the boat scraped against the jetty, and groaned. 'Just get me something for this head, it's making me feel sick!'

'We're here now—the doctor will see you.'

He opened his eyes again and looked at the dusty, sprawling village with its few thin trees and squat stone houses, and pulled a face. 'It isn't exactly Istan-bul, is it?'

Tatlisu might have lacked size and modernity, but there were willing male hands soon available when the boat's owner called for assistance to get his passenger ashore, and Ian was half carried by two of the men, followed by a dozen more, solemn-faced and already involved in the rescue as far as interest was concerned.

There was a brief discussion in Turkish while the two main members of the party gently carried Ian on their clasped hands, and without pause they all trooped in the direction of a house that stood at one end of the village, a slightly larger house than the rest, but with the usual outside staircase and squat tiled roof.

It was the doctor's house, Laurette assumed, and the ceremony of knocking was dispensed with. The door was simply pushed open and the whole party went in-side, closing the door behind them, leaving Laurette on the outside. It was the normal thing to do, of course, the men would not even think about Ian preferring her to be there too, women had no place in this particular episode.

There were women about, naturally curious, but they satisfied their interest from a distance, dark-eyed looks directed at her from above the illegal but still widely used veil. It was not a veil strictly speaking, but simply an extension of the headcloth worn by the women, drawn across the lower half of the face, so that it was difficult to tell who might be smiling without being able to see their mouths.

A large and bony dog showed an interest, sniffing around her ankles, and a small boy hurled a handful of dirt from the road to discourage it, a gesture that seemed to spark sudden life into the watching women. One of them came forward, younger than the rest, Laurette thought, letting the concealing cloth fall from her face as she came and smiling, her large dark eyes shyly friendly.

'*Müsade edin, hanim*, I have English a little. May we offer you *çay*?'

Laurette smiled gratefully. Whoever had said that the English are the race who solve all their problems with a cup of tea had never visited Turkey! The offer of tea was inevitable, like the hospitality that prompted it.

'That's very kind of you, thank you.' She repeated her thanks in Turkish, and the woman looked delighted, as if she had paid her a personal compliment, remarking on it to her friends. 'But first,' Laurette went on, wondering just how good the woman's English was, 'I must find a telephone. *Telefon etmek istiyorum*—I have to make a telephone call.'

'*Telefon*?' Her informant looked vaguely puzzled.

96

She had never used the instrument herself, nor had any of her friends. 'The house of the *doktor* has the *telefon, hanim.*'

It made sense, of course, for who else in a village this size would have need of such sophistication? Laurette glanced over her shoulder at the doctor's house, which must already be full to overflowing with Ian and his rescuers, and pulled a face. 'Then I'm going to have to ask the doctor if I can use that one.'

Obviously the idea caused something of a stir among the women, for they were looking at her curiously, and rather as if she was some kind of privileged person. 'You can use *telefon, hanim?*'

Laurette did not look forward to making her way through a crowd of men to do so, but she had no choice it seemed, and she smiled ruefully. 'I have to,' she said, and hoped the doctor proved sufficiently enlightened to allow her the privilege. 'But I'll be very grateful for that tea when I come back.'

'*Evet, hanim.*'

Clearly her bravado intrigued them, for they watched her all the way to the doctor's house, where it sat in the shade of a plane tree, closed and seemingly silent until she first knocked tentatively and then pushed open the door. At once a deep rumble of male conversation met her, ceasing abruptly when she walked in.

Ian must be alone with the doctor somewhere, for there was no sign of him among the group of men who turned as one and regarded her curiously. Putting on a bold face, she sought and found a door with a neat brass plate that spelled out *klinik*, which was as near to surgery as she was likely to get, she thought.

Her tentative knock was answered after a second or two by a young man in a white coat, who looked at her for a moment as if he did not quite believe he was see-

97

ing her. Recalling himself suddenly, he smiled and inclined his head, inviting her in.

The surgery was neat and spotlessly clean, and surprisingly well equipped, smelling of the same curious mixture of smells that surgeries anywhere in the world smelled of. She stood for a moment, her expression showing her surprise, and aware that the doctor was regarding her in a way that seemed to suggest he recognised her. Though how, she could not imagine.

'You seek reassurance, *hanim*?'

He would know she had been left outside, of course, but he understood how she felt, which the men outside probably did not. 'I wondered if—I'm sorry, doctor, I should have introduced myself. My name's Laurette Kearn.'

'Ah, yes, of course—Miss Kearn!' He spoke excellent English and offered his hand. 'I am Sadi Teoman, Miss Kearn.'

Ian had evidently given him her name, and she thanked heaven he was apparently very progressive. His handshake and his smile were both friendly and uninhibited, and she was grateful for it. 'I'm so glad you speak such good English, doctor.' She laughed a little uncertainly and glanced at Ian on a small bed that evidently did service as an examination couch. He appeared to be too ill to take any interest in her sudden appearance, and she felt more concerned than ever. 'How's Ian?'

'My patient?' The doctor smiled reassuringly. 'Oh, he'll be fine in a few days, though he is not feeling very good at the moment, I am afraid.'

'Poor Ian.' She smiled at him gratefully, though she was still puzzled as to why an apparently well educated and progressive man should choose to bury himself in

98

a village the size of Tatlisu. 'I'm thankful he's in good hands, doctor.'

His eyes had a darkly mischievous look that was very attractive and he showed excellent teeth in another smile. 'But it surprises you to find such—good hands in a village like Tatlisu?' He obviously enjoyed her surprise and made no secret of it. 'I was trained in a London hospital, Miss Kearn, but I was born not far from here. I was one of the lucky ones, and I am here because I am grateful for that.'

'Oh, I see—well, it's lucky for us that you are here, doctor. But I wonder if I could impose further on your time by asking to use your telephone. It's the only one in the village, I believe.'

'Oh, but of course! Will you come with me?'

The telephone was in another room, one that appeared to be used as an office, and led off the surgery. He indicated the instrument standing on a desk by the window, but did not leave her, as she expected. Instead he was regarding her curiously. 'Forgive my curiosity, Miss Kearn, but you are the lady who is—in the care of the Kayaman family, are you not?'

His knowledge was unexpected, and his delicate wording of her position in the family was typical of someone uncertain of his ground, so that she looked at him for a second or two before she replied. 'I'm Refik Bey's foster-daughter, in fact, Doctor Teoman. Do you know him?'

The doctor nodded, one finger rubbing his chin thoughtfully. 'I know Refik Bey slightly—I know Nuri Kayaman better; we were at university together and we still have contact quite frequently.'

'Oh!' Heaven knew why she coloured up the way she did, but the doctor noted the fact with interest, she thought. It was ridiculous how sensitive she had become about Nuri lately. 'I didn't realise that.'

'It is quite possible,' Doctor Teoman acknowledged, with a smile for his country's traditions. 'Nuri's sisters would know few of his male friends, even his foster-sister.'

'That's true.' She put a hand on the telephone, recalling her need of it. 'I want to call Yarev, actually, and get someone to come and fetch us. I thought it was a better idea than letting Ian struggle on and off a boat, the way we came.'

'Much better,' the doctor agreed, his dark eyes frankly curious. 'I am sure that Nuri would be only too pleased to drive you—and your friend—home.'

'Ian's my cousin.'

'Ah!' He smiled and touched his own dark hair. 'The red hair—it is very distinctive.'

'We only recently met, and discovered each other. Three nights ago, in fact. It was rather exciting to find I had someone of my own.'

'Naturally. I was rather surprised when I learned who you were to see you with a young man.' He was smiling; a nice, friendly, but unreservedly admiring smile that brought a faint flush to her cheeks. 'My friend Kayaman is quite right—you are a very lovely young woman, they have need to take good care of you.'

The flush in her cheeks became a bright pink warmth there was no concealing, and she hastily avoided the doctor's speculative eyes. 'Nuri—said that?'

Doctor Teoman was smiling, she could tell from the sound of his voice, even though she did not look at him again. 'I have been indiscreet,' he mourned. 'I hope you will not let Nuri know that I have what your country-men would call—put my foot in it. You will not give me away, hmm?'

'No, of course not.'

100

He did not really expect her to, she thought, but the idea of Nuri talking about her to his friends gave her a curious feeling, and she was not sure whether or not she liked it. His description of her had been flattering, at least according to the doctor, and that was something she could not take exception to—in fact she rather liked the idea of that.

She found the matter more immediately compelling than making her call, and Doctor Teoman was watching her closely from the other side of the desk, obviously sensing something of what was in her mind. 'Turkish men are not so very different from Englishmen, Miss Kearn. When we are together we discuss women. Among other subjects, of course,' he added with a wry smile. 'But I promise you that you have never been the subject of any—uncomplimentary or improper conversation.' The dark eyes held hers steadily for a moment, and were too honest and too unwavering not to be believed. 'Your foster-brother is very—fond of you, of that I can assure you.'

'I know.' Laurette hastily avoided his eyes and lifted the receiver from its rest. 'I'll see if someone can come and fetch us—if Nuri has arrived home by now, he might come.'

'And if he does, you will not tell him that I have been indiscreet?'

Laurette was not sure just how serious his plea was, but she smiled at him reassuringly and shook her head. 'I promise.'

Knowing that Ian was in good hands with Doctor Teoman, Laurette had no reason to worry about him for the moment, so while she waited for Refik Kayaman to come for them in a car she took advantage of the offer to have tea. She had never yet visited a house in a real country district, and she quite looked forward to the experience.

Her hostess, as it turned out, lived in one of the larger houses. It was double-storied, not single, and little more than a hut, as some of them were. It stood in the centre of the village, not too far from the doctor's house should she be needed, and had the usual outside staircase giving access to the upper floor where the living quarters were.

It was to be a party, it seemed, for several of the other women joined her and her hostess, all removing their shoes in the customary way before entering. Her hostess, she learned, was called Suna Melen and her husband, Ismail, was among those at the doctor's house. He was, so Suna confided with some pride, a progressive man who allowed her more freedom than most of the men allowed their wives, an opinion that none of the other women saw fit to debate, so it was probably true.

Laurette was solemnly introduced to the rest in strict order of seniority as was customary, and they seated themselves in a circle around their guest. The room was neat and clean, and furnished with hard, flat cushions set on the thinly carpeted floor; cushions that Laurette found much less comfortable than the fat feathery comfort of the ottoman at home. Wooden chests standing around the walls contained the family's bedding, neatly stored away for the day, and the room was surprisingly cool considering the wood-burning stove that gave off a smoky and slightly perfumed smell.

The traditional round tray-like table set on low legs was brought and set in the centre of the group of women, but talk was sparse at first. Only one other beside Suna Melen spoke a little English, and the ones who did not were too polite to converse in their own

102

tongue when their visitor could not be included in their conversation.

It caused them no frustration to sit silently, however, for they were accustomed to doing so whenever their menfolk talked together, and a great deal could be conveyed simply by using their expressive dark eyes and a series of vague fluttering gestures. It was a form of communication that reminded her in some way of Halet and her sisters, and it occurred to her that possibly it was one developed by generations of women who spoke only when they were spoken to, and then softly and briefly, so as not to intrude.

Veils were lowered in the house where there was no one but women, and Laurette set the conversational ball rolling by asking about the tea they were drinking and the method of brewing it. At Yarev she was accustomed to a samovar being used, but here it was different. The tea had a curious herbal taste that she was told came from the leaves of the linden, called *thlamur*, and it was brewed by placing a small kettle containing the tea on top of a large enamel one, where the lid would normally sit.

It was almost a ritual, as so many Turkish pleasures were, and the finished brew, served in their hostess's best glass goblets and thick with sugar, was definitely an acquired taste. With the serving of tea tongues were loosened, and questions began, tentative at first in the polite Turkish way, and then increasingly searching when the subject showed no sign of resentment at their interest, and all very formally translated by Suna Melen, whose English, it appeared, was rather better than it had seemed at first.

The Turks were a very sociable race and in this little out-of-the-way village there would seldom if ever be a stranger to break the monotony of the everyday round.

103

One of the older women asked something and Suna Melen translated it solemnly for her.

'Nilufer Hanim asks if your brother is very ill, *hanim*.'

Laurette smiled her thanks for the enquiry, fully aware that such an assumption was inevitable in the circumstances, and would not be as straight forward to deny as might be supposed. 'Oh, he has only a touch of sunstroke. *Günes çarpmasi*—he'll be better in a few days, thank you. But he isn't my brother, he's my cousin —*kuzen*.'

'Not your brother?'

It was clear that her interpreter hesitated to pass on such a surprising piece of news, and Laurette could feel shrewd dark eyes questioning the delay. Another question prompted her and was answered at once, the news that Ian's illness was not too serious, apparently, since the old head nodded satisfaction.

The situation was different, however, when more slowly and with obvious hesitation, the rest of the information was passed on, and the older woman frowned at Laurette curiously, unwilling to believe what she heard, it seemed.

'Nilufer says that she can then assume you to be betrothed to the man with red hair, *hanim*.' She hurried on, as if she feared Laurette might think her as unprogressive as her neighbour. 'The older women do not have the understanding, you see, *hanim*.'

'No, of course they don't.' Laurette was determinedly casual about it, but she suspected that even the progressive Suna was a little taken aback at such boldness. 'It's quite normal among my people for men and women to go about together, but tell Nilufer Hanim that I belong to—that I live with a Turkish family, and I understand her reaction.'

The message was passed on and the old woman once

more expressed surprise, but the question Suna Melen asked next was to satisfy her own curiosity, Laurette thought. 'You live in Turkey, *hanim*? You like our country?'

A Turk always knew the answer to that one, but Suna Melen waited smilingly for it to be confirmed. 'I love it,' Laurette said sincerely. 'I live in Antalya with a family called Kayaman and I've been with them for so long now that I feel myself Turkish by now.'

It was a compliment that Suna appreciated and translated willingly for her friends. There were smiles all round, with one exception—the old woman, Nilufer, who was still not satisfied and made little attempt to conceal the fact. It seemed the name Kayaman meant something to her too, which was not really surprising, for the family firm was well known in the area and could easily have reached this village too, but whatever she said, Suna Melen was obviously less pleased to translate.

'Is something wrong?'

Laurette asked the question to ease the way for her interpreter, for she was so evidently unwilling to pass on whatever it was the old woman had said to her. 'Such things are not for talk with strangers, *hanim*. I will not insult you by repeating them.'

She looked so defiantly at the older woman, that Laurette was inevitably intrigued to know what was too awful to be translated for her ears. Her smattering of Turkish informed her that it concerned someone's cousin and the Kayaman family, but she could not be left in this unsatisfying state of limbo, and pleaded with her hostess to overcome her sensitivity and tell her.

With much glancing at the old woman from the corners of her eyes, the reluctant Suna did so. 'Nilufer saye she has knowledge of the family Kayaman, *hanim*,

105

through a cousin who has a friend in the house of Refik Bey as a servant.'

From that somewhat complex situation Laurette gathered that the old woman's cousin had been gossiping as people do the world over, about her employer and his family, but what puzzled her was what she could possibly have heard that could cause the sharp look on that wrinkled brown face opposite. Something that Suna Melen was not happy about translating.

She smiled, showing that she could think of nothing to arouse such untypical malice, and made her answer to Suna. 'Then Nilufer Hanim will know that I come from a very fine home and good people,' she said, an answer which Suna translated willingly. 'Perhaps I can hear what it is that's causing her such concern. Won't you please tell me?'

She had a curious sense of anticipation in the pit of her stomach and waited. The young woman was not happy about it, but she could not refuse to oblige a guest and she did so in a low soft voice that made her dislike of the situation quite clear.

'Forgive me, *hanim*, but Nilufer is of the mind that you have—run away with this man who has *günes çarpmasi*. Our men would not allow us to entertain a woman who has done this.'

'No, of course not.' Laurette accepted the statement at its face value, knowing it would be a serious matter among these people, but she was still puzzled. 'But why on earth should she think I've run away? I'm very happy at home.'

'This cousin is a speaker of gossip,' Suna Melen informed her, safe in the knowledge that old Nilufer could not understand and contradict. 'It has been told that there is to be a betrothal, *hanim*, between the son of Refik Bey and the woman upon whom he looks as a

106

daughter. It is from this betrothal that Nilufer says you run.'

Laurette was shaking her head slowly back and forth, too stunned for the moment to find words. Her heart was hammering against her ribs like a drum beat suddenly and she looked at her informant with wide, unbelieving eyes. She did not know what she had expected to hear when she pressed Suna Melen to tell her what the old woman had said, but certainly nothing like this.

She was the centre of all eyes, but it was Suna Melen who was their combined voice. 'It is a bad idea, *hanim*?'

'It's a *wrong* idea!' Laurette corrected her automatically. 'I can't think how on earth she got hold of such a—a silly story!'

There were all too many surprises happening lately, concerning Nuri and herself. Latife's suggestion that he was jealous of her being in the garden so long with Ian; Doctor Teoman's reference to the flattering way Nuri spoke of her, even Nuri's own unaccustomed familiarity—and now this. It was no more than servants' gossip, of course, but there were far too many misconceptions abroad, and she really ought to do something about putting a stop to them.

Suna Melen was kneeling beside her, refilling the goblet she held with steamingly fragrant tea, and looking at her curiously as she did so. 'There is no betrothal, *hanim*?' She sounded almost disappointed, and in other circumstances Laurette might have laughed, as she had done at Halet more than once in similar situations. Only this, somehow, was more serious and it made her strangely uneasy in this company of strangers.

'Definitely not!'

She kept a firm hold on her impulses, and held the glass goblet tightly between her hands, inhaling the fragrance of its contents and firmly suppressing the instinct she had to get up and leave. She must surely have become more Turkish than she realised over the past few years, for she managed to conceal her inner turmoil with a veneer of coolness that probably fooled at least some of her companions.

Just as the rest did, she turned her head swiftly when a man's voice called from the foot of the stairs to his wife, and Suna Melen rose hastily to her feet to answer it. Whatever news he imparted it had the women reaching to draw their veils across their faces once more, and their dark eyes above them, looked at Laurette with renewed interest. The old woman, Nilufer, muttered something behind the muffling cloth, and Suna Melen turned, her eyes too, speculative.

'Nuri Bey is here to take you back, *hanim*.'

Old Nilufer nodded her satisfaction when Laurette got to her feet, though much less hastily than Suna had answered her husband's call, and it was possible she suspected just how urgently Laurette's heart was beating as she stood for a moment brushing down her skirt.

She had expected Baba Refik to come, as he had promised; why did it have to be Nuri? And the way Suna Melen had worded it—Nuri Bey is here to take you back—how could she expect these women to believe anything else than that he had come in anger because she had gone off with another man? She smiled at Suna Melen and nodded, her expression giving no clue to the turmoil that was going on in her mind.

'I'll say goodbye to the ladies and join him in a few moments,' she said. 'Will you ask your husband to tell him that, please, Suna Hanim?'

The request was complied with somewhat dubiously, then Suna stood at the top of the stairs with her veil drawn across her face and her eyes watching for the man who had come to fetch their visitor. He appeared

108

at the same moment Laurette shook hands with her hostess, a tall, commanding figure who tipped back his head to look up and hid the expression in his eyes with thick black lashes.

'Laurette?'

He waited while she came down the wooden stairs, then stood for a moment after she joined him, looking down at her. 'It was good of you to come, Nuri.' She made her voice as light and casual as she could, and he took her arm without answering, steering her across to where his car was parked in the dusty street surrounded by admiring men.

Ian was on the back seat, lying full length and with his head supported by a cushion, much more relaxed than when she had seen him last and perhaps slightly less flushed. The door was open and she got in beside him, brushing back the hair from his brow and noticing that it was much less chilled and damp.

'Ian, are you feeling better?'

'I suppose so—the doc says I am.'

He made the admission grudgingly, and she realised he was probably drowsy after some injection or other he had been given. He had opened his eyes only briefly, but managed to frown when he saw Nuri standing just behind her. She had not closed the door and she expected him to do it, squatting back on her heels when he did not and looking at him warily.

'I expected Baba Refik to come, but——'

'I was already in my car, it was the simplest thing for me to come instead.' He seemed to be waiting for her to leave Ian and ride in front with him, and she was in two minds about it. 'When you are ready we will go.'

'Yes, of course. I'll ride in the back with Ian.'

'Your cousin has been advised to lie still and full length on the seat,' Nuri told her shortly. 'It will be much simpler and more comfortable if you ride with me, Laurette.'

Ian had his eyes partly open again and he was watching her, not trying to persuade her, but watching to see what she would do, and she had the feeling somehow that the men standing around were waiting for her to decide as well. She could insist on staying with Ian, although there was not really room for her, or she could ride with Nuri up front, as he said. That, she realised, surrounded by all those dark, male faces, was what she was expected to do.

'Yes, of course,' she said. 'Then Ian can rest.'

She got out of the car and Nuri's strong fingers guided her into the front passenger seat, squeezing gently just before they released her, and when she looked up at him briefly, his black eyes had a deep dark glow in their depths that set her pulse racing.

Nuri Bey is here to take you back, was the message Suna Melen had delivered, and when she caught a glimpse of several pairs of dark eyes watching from the upper windows of the house she had just left, she had the strangest feeling that it was they who had put the right interpretation on the message after all.

CHAPTER SIX

IT went very much against the grain to leave Ian alone in his hotel bedroom, but he firmly refused to take advantage of an invitation to stay at Yarev until he was recovered. His refusal, Laurette suspected, stemmed from the fact that although Nuri had issued the invitation on behalf of his father, he left little doubt that whether he appeared inhospitable or not, he had no enthusiasm for the idea. Refik Kayaman would have been happier, if only for Laurette's sake, but he would not insist, for to pressure a man into accepting hospitality he did not wish to accept was as impolite as not to offer it at all.

In her concern for Ian it had been easy to forget the circumstances that had led to their going on that boat trip in the first place, and she had not given another thought to Nuri having seen them at the theatre. She visited Ian at his hotel, and determinedly ignored the questioning looks of the desk clerk. Ian was her cousin and she had to stand by him, even if only for that reason.

The sickness, as Doctor Teoman had forecast, soon diminished, and by the second day Ian was talking about getting up. What would happen after that she had no clear idea, but he could hardly go out and about in the sun for a while, which was going to restrict their activities. However, that was something they could discuss this morning while they sat in the hotel gardens under the trees, which was where she had arranged to meet him.

Coming downstairs she felt quite lighthearted, a mood inspired in part by a new silk dress she was wearing, and which made her feel rather special. Its colour was the same soft bluey-green as the ocean below the cliffs in the harbour, and with her copper-red hair it was dazzlingly effective. Watching the way the skirt swished about her legs as she came downstairs, she smiled to herself a bit complacently, unaware of being watched until a voice snatched her out of her mood.

'Laurette?'

Nuri stood just outside the door of the *salon*, as if he had just left it, and she viewed his sudden appearance with mixed feelings. She had seen very little of him in the past couple of days, not exactly by design, although she supposed subconsciously she had tried not to see him too often. There was something about the way he watched her come down the last few stairs that brought old Nilufer's suspicions to mind, and she felt strangely uneasy with that black-eyed gaze on her.

'Will you speak with me for a few moments?'

As if she stood much chance of refusing! She pushed her hair back from her face with a vague hand and nodded as she came down into the hall. 'Yes, of course, Nuri.'

He stood holding open the door of the *salon*, just as he had on the last occasion when they had talked alone in the *salon*, she recalled, and found the recollection discomfiting. That time he had kissed her, unexpectedly and with devastating effect, and she remembered the fact with a wildly thudding heartbeat.

It was doubtful if he had anything as unexpected in mind for this interview, but she could do nothing about the curious sense of anticipation that curled in her

112

stomach as she approached him. In fact he looked far more as if he meant to censure her for something, and she sought hastily among her recent misdemeanours for something to account for it. The angle of her chin as she passed him in the doorway was quite unconsciously challenging and she hated it because she knew her cheeks coloured furiously.

'You're going to tell me off, aren't you?'

He would dislike the direct challenge, that went without saying and she felt her pulses flutter alarmingly in response to the touch of her bare arm in brief contact with the hard vigour of him. It was a new experience, being so very aware of him as a man, and she found it very hard to cope with at the moment.

'I wish you wouldn't, Nuri. It simply means that we shall fight again, and I really don't want to fight with you.'

Close on her heels as she crossed to her favourite seat on the ottoman, he watched her tuck her legs up under her as she always did. 'I find that hard to believe,' he said, 'since you seem to go out of your way to create the situations. Sometimes I think you actually enjoy quarrelling with me.'

'Oh, but I *don't*!'

She looked up swiftly to deny it, and something in his manner as he stood over her, looking down from his superior height, reminded her once more of that last time they had been alone together in this room, and she shivered. He noticed, and a black brow commented, but that was all.

He did not sit beside her as she anticipated, but chose instead to occupy one of the armchairs, leaning back in it and crossing his long legs, as if he was completely relaxed, when she felt quite sure he was not. There were signs, things she recognised after long ex-

113

perience, that meant he was either angry or uneasy about something, and she looked at him curiously from the concealment of her lashes.

Taking out one of the long Turkish cigarettes he smoked, he lit it before he spoke again, but it was so seldom that he smoked in her company that she could not help showing her surprise. Once more he noted her reaction, and looking at the cigarette between his long fingers, he inclined his head in a curiously formal apology.

'You have no objection if I smoke?'

'No, of course not.'

His black eyes, narrowed behind the drifting smoke, were regarding her steadily. 'But of course you will be more accustomed to the habit now that you see so much more of your cousin, will you not?'

'I'm used to Ian smoking, if that's what you mean.' Her hands clenched, she looked at him and frowned. 'But if you're referring to Ian why don't you use his name, Nuri? Surely you don't dislike him that much, do you?'

It took her only a moment to recognise that she had already made what could well be the first step towards another scene with him, and she bit her lip anxiously, trying to draw back before it was too late. Another long draw at the cigarette preceded a smoke screen that all but hid his face from her, so it was difficult to judge his reaction, but his words were cool and quiet, his words startling.

'I dislike anyone who can persuade you to deceive your family, and particularly my father.'

'Oh, Nuri, that really isn't fair!'

But it was fair as far as he was concerned, she realised with dismay. All her good intentions of telling her foster-father about the unexpected visit to the theatre

114

to see the wrestling had gone by the board in the past couple of days, and it had been left to Nuri to remind her.

To him it must look very much as if she had simply sneaked off with Ian and intended keeping quiet about it, except that Nuri had seen them and made that impossible. She scarcely expected him to believe her good intention now. What puzzled her as much as anything was her own present reaction to his reminder.

Normally she would have been angry at his bringing it to her attention, but instead she felt rather small and guilty because she had allowed her involvement with Ian to let her forget about everything else. And the persistent memory of the last time they had been alone together, and the way he had kissed her, undermined her anger in a way she found hard to understand.

'I didn't deceive anyone, Nuri—not deliberately.'

'No?'

She met his eyes for a second only, trying to discover just how implacable he was behind that concealing screen of smoke that hid his expression from her and softened the chiselled, hawk-like features. Hands open on her lap and palms upward, she spoke quietly and without anger.

'I meant to tell Baba Refik as soon as I got home, Nuri, but with Ian being taken ill and then——' She shrugged helplessly. 'It slipped my mind, that's all.' Her expression was anxious suddenly. 'You haven't told him, have you, Nuri?'

A swirling jet of smoke issued between pursed lips and he regarded her through the resultant cloud for a second. 'You have to ask me that?'

'That's right—you never told tales on us, did you?'

He could have done so many times, she thought, but she had never before stopped to reason his motive for not doing so. She had assumed in the past that it had been done with the idea of protecting her and Halet from his father's displeasure. Now it seemed possible that the reverse was possibly true—that he protected his father from the annoyance of their misdemeanours. He had a great love for his father, as well as respect.

She received no reply to her question, but the black eyes were fixed on her unwaveringly behind that smoke screen he created. 'I had not seen you capable of deliberately deceiving my father, though I know you would deceive me and take pleasure in my finding out, if you knew it would anger me.'

'Oh, no, I——'

A raised hand stilled her protest, his wide mouth distorted with a wry half-smile. 'Why deny it, *bebek*? You would do almost anything if you thought it would —what is it?—get a rise out of me!'

The unaccustomed slang sounded clumsy on his pedantic tongue, but she was more dismayed at his opinion of her than she would have believed possible. She sat for a moment or two with her hands in her lap, restless fingers alternately pleating and smoothing the hem of her dress and not looking at him, but very conscious of the black gaze watching her.

Her mouth looked unusually soft and vulnerable; not sulky, but reproachful, and she thought of all the times when she would have flown into a temper if he had been only half as provoking as he was being now. Why she was taking it so meekly, she had no idea, and there was a certain gleam in Nuri's black eyes that suggested he too was intrigued by the new state of affairs.

'I—I didn't realise you had quite such a low opinion of me.'

The sound of her own voice dismayed her, for it was breathless and husky, as if she was on the brink of tears, and when she looked across at him her eyes showed the same symptoms—bright and suspiciously misty, a situation she was at a loss to account for. Crossing swords with Nuri was hardly a novel experience, but she had seldom shed tears over it, yet she felt very much as if she wanted to at this moment.

'So it *was* because you wanted to tell me off that you asked me to come in here!' She laughed, very unsteadily, and shook her head, resigned to the inevitable. 'I knew it had to be—how could it be anything else?'

'Laurette——'

'Oh, please don't say any more! You've achieved your object, Nuri! I'll go and see Baba Refik, duly chastened and put firmly in my place by my big brother!' She got to her feet and wished her legs felt less shaky, and her voice was more firmly confident. 'But you reminded me, Nuri, that's all. No matter what you choose to believe, I *was* going to tell Baba Refik all about it; he'll know that I would have told him first if I'd——'

'You did not know you were going!' His black eyes searched over her face, seeking confirmation. 'You did not know *where* Ian Kearn was taking you when you left here, that is why you did not say anything!'

There was no concealing the fact that only now did he recognise the fact, and it hurt to see him admit it. He really had thought she was deceiving his father and going to places she knew he would not like her visiting. Thrusting out her chin, she looked at him from the shadow of her thick lashes, as near anger as she had yet come, yet still more hurt than angry, and puzzled by the fact.

'You really believed I'd—I'd sneaked in there without saying anything, didn't you? You actually thought I was capable of being that deceitful!'

117

'Laurette, please listen to me.'

He was on his feet with one large hand on her arm until she snatched it away and stood blinking at him with eyes that were now so close to tears that they looked diamond-bright in her flushed face. Turning swiftly before he had time to say anything more, she hurried across the room away from him; in search of his father. Someone who would believe and understand her —Nuri never would.

Whether he started to follow her, or even if he called after her, she had no idea, for her head was pounding with some violent emotion she was incapable of controlling at the moment. Refik Kayaman had an office-study on the ground floor, and she made her way there on legs that trembled so much she feared they might not carry her that far.

This seemed so much more important than her usual disagreements with Nuri, and yet she could think of no reason why it should be. It seemed a kind of climax, as if things were suddenly coming to a head, and she wished she felt more able to cope. If she had to go, if she had to leave Yarev, now was as good a time as any. That was the thought that beat relentlessly in her brain as she raised her hand to knock on the door, and it brought with it a kind of panic, for everything seemed to be going much too fast suddenly.

'Girl'

Laurette opened the door cautiously in response to the invitation. It was a room she had been into no more than a couple of times in all the years she had been at Yarev, for it was her foster-father's private sanctum, and she had a moment's doubt whether or not she should have chosen to visit him there.

But Refik Kayaman was holding out his hands to her, almost as if she was expected, his shrewd but kindly

118

eyes taking note of her flushed cheeks and the tears that trembled on thick brown lashes. Taking her hands, he held her gently for a moment, and from his expression of mingled regret and resignation, she knew he had already delegated the blame for her tears.

'What is it, *bebek*, hmm?'

'Could I see you for a few moments, Baba Refik?' A hard swallow was an attempt to steady her voice, though it achieved little in the way of relief. 'I—I want to tell you something I should have——' She shook her head and looked at him appealingly. 'If I'm not being a pest.'

'A pest! Dear child, how often have I heard your father use that curious word to chide you!' His smile was reassuring, and already the problems that had oppressed her seemed a little less overwhelming. 'You wish to tell me what is troubling you, hmm?' He distorted his strong features into a grimace in an attempt to make her smile. 'Or is it that you have quarrelled with Nuri yet again, little one?'

'Well—yes, I have, but that isn't really what I want to talk to you about, Baba Refik.'

'Ah! Then sit with me and we will have *çay* while we talk, hmm?'

A samovar stood on a small table and the steaming fragrance of tea was irresistible as a nerve-soother, so Laurette nodded her thanks. Sitting on an ottoman similar to the one in the *salon*, she chose a more conventional attitude in this instance, sitting with her feet on the floor and her hands in her lap, until a goblet of tea was pushed gently into her fingers.

Refik Kayaman sat beside her, his dark face carefully composed so as not to show any expression but gentle enquiry, a look that was reflected in his eyes as he sipped his tea. He would not think of putting pressure on her to hurry because he had other things to do

—not Baba Refik. He would listen to her patiently and tolerantly, not simply for her father's sake now, but because he had come to love her almost as much as he did his own daughters.

Soothed in part by the tea, Laurette put down her glass carefully on the table beside her, feeling much more composed. First she would tell him about Aspendus, the rest could come later. He would find it hard to understand why she saw the need to leave Yarev before it was absolutely necessary, and she was not sure herself if she understood her reasons.

'Baba Refik, I would have told you before if I'd known I was going, and I meant to mention it when I came back, only Ian was ill, and——'

'*Yavas, yavas, bebek!* Go more slowly—you refer to the fact that your cousin took you to see wrestling in the theatre at Aspendus, is that right?' His voice was quiet, soothing, and when she looked at him there was a gentle look of laughter in his eyes.

'Nuri didn't tell you?'

She waited anxiously for his confirmation, and when he shook his head she had no idea of the look of relief that passed across her face. 'Laurette, you must know Nuri better than that by now. I will not believe otherwise!'

'No, of course he wouldn't tell you. But he was so——' She shrugged helplessly and once more the threat of tears brought a huskiness to her voice that she could do nothing about. 'Baba, he really believed that I'd deceived you! That I'd gone there with Ian and deliberately not told you because I knew you wouldn't like it.'

'Oh no, little one. No, no, no, I will not believe that!'

'But he *did*!' She could still look stunned at the idea of it being possible. 'I saw his face; he thought I'd been

120

deliberately—sneaky. How *could* he, Baba Refik?'

A brown hand stroked the hair from her forehead, and the old man's eyes were gently understanding. 'Perhaps because he is—confused, child. He is not as confident that he has everything perfectly in perspective and under control at the moment, and to a man like Nuri such a situation is unbearable.'

'Nuri? Confused? I don't understand.'

'No, *bebek*, I do not think you do.' He put a hand at the back of her head and drew her close enough to place a light kiss on her brow. 'It is something that will become clearer with time.' He handed her his glass goblet to be refilled from the samovar and she automatically took over the role that women commonly fulfilled in his world. 'Now we will have more *çay* and you will tell me what else it is that troubles you, hmm?'

She handed him his tea, casting a curious glance from below thick brown lashes. 'If Nuri didn't tell you about my being at the wrestling, Baba Refik, who did?'

Refik Kayaman sipped his tea slowly and smiled. 'I have friends who like to watch wrestling, *bebek*. You were seen by one of them and he thought it his place to inform me of the fact. He was—surprised to see you there, and I was not inclined to let him know that I had no knowledge of it, so that I am afraid he now thinks of me as rather more progressive than he had realised.'

'Oh, Baba Refik, I'm sorry if it embarrassed you! I would have told you before I went, if I'd known, and I meant to tell you when I came back, whether Nuri believes it or not.'

'I knew you would, child, and it is understandable that you forget in the confusion of your cousin being taken ill.' He put down his glass on the small table beside him, then looked at her searchingly for a second

121

or two. 'This cousin, *bebek*, he is a man who does not like our country?'

It was delicately worded, but Laurette could guess the meaning behind the question, and she hastily sought to deny that Ian disliked Turkey and the Turks. She firmly believed he did not—only Nuri really invoked his anger and his dislike, and that was because he considered Nuri kept far too sharp an eye on her.

'Oh, Ian likes it here, Baba Refik, and he likes the people.'

'But he does not perhaps approve of our customs, hmm?'

'Not always.' She admitted it with a curious reluctance, because the next step was to suppose that he would try and influence her in to his way of thinking. 'He isn't used to us yet, but I'm trying to explain things as best I can.'

Refik Kayaman's dark eyes searched her face slowly, with a look of infinite gentleness, then he smiled in a way that tugged at her heart-strings without her quite knowing why, until he spoke. 'He would take you away from us, little one, eh?'

'Oh, Baba Refik, no! I promise I won't——'

She broke off hastily when she remembered that soon now she would have to go. At least away from Yarev when Halet married. Nuri had already gone into the question of proprieties, but she wondered if her foster-father had. It would be impossible for her to bring up the matter of her leaving before she needed to now, and she shook her head while Refik Kayaman watched her and sipped his tea once more.

'When Halet and Hussein marry, of course I'll have to leave, but I'm hoping to find somewhere quite close by.'

It was only seeing his surprise that made Laurette

122

realise he had assumed the deduction was her own. He was half smiling and nodding his head, and she let the assumption go on for a while. 'You have the wisdom to see that such a move is inevitable, Laurette, that is well, though we shall grieve to have you leave us. Somewhere will be found for you, close by, as you say. Perhaps with Latife and Furedin—until you marry.'

A swift disturbing flutter stirred in her breast and she looked at him covertly, wondering if he had already discussed the matter of a husband with Nuri. Nuri's own remarks on the subject seemed to suggest it, and she once more felt that same instinctive dislike of the idea. Her voice determinedly steady, she shook her head.

'I've already told Nuri that I'm not interested in marriage as a solution, Baba Refik.'

Completely taken by surprise, Refik Kayaman looked as fiercely disapproving as ever his son had, and she realised too late how wrong she had been to mention it. To her foster-father the idea of Nuri discussing her marriage plans with her was unthinkable, and she had made him angry with his son, quite unthinkingly.

'Nuri has dared to discuss the matter with you?' He gave her no time to confirm or deny it, but went on, leaving his opinion in no doubt at all, 'He has no right to take such a matter upon himself, Laurette, and I shall let him know of my displeasure!'

Appalled at the very idea, she shook her head urgently, her eyes wide and appealing. 'Oh no, please don't do that, Baba Refik! Don't let him know that I've told you! It wasn't at all like you think, and he really hasn't done anything wrong.'

The old man's dark eyes regarded her for a moment, and his brows were drawn. 'He was wrong to discuss such matters with you, little one, you must know that.'

'I know, but——' Words did not come easily, but she had to admit to provoking Nuri to some extent, though she doubted if his father would see it as an excuse. 'It was my fault in a way, Baba Refik. I—I made him angry and——' Shrugging helplessly, she looked at the kind but stern face appealingly. 'He'll hate it if he knows I've told you,' she pleaded. 'Please don't mention it to him, Baba Refik.'

Slowly the dark eyes searched her face, gentling with understanding even while he still studied her. Then he smiled and slowly shook his head. 'And it would not do for Nuri to hate what you do, would it, *bebek*?' Gentle fingers stroked her cheek. 'Very well, I will do as you ask and not let him know how displeased I am with his behaviour, since it is so important to you.'

'Oh, thank you!'

It was impossible to disguise her relief, and the old man regarded her with the same knowing look while he held out his glass for more tea. 'He should see how anxiously and earnestly you appeal for him, little one! What would he have to say to that?'

Pouring herself more tea so that a bent head could hide at least most of her face and the flush on her cheeks was not too obvious, she laughed a little wildly. 'Oh, he'd probably say I was doing it for my own ends, and in a way I suppose he's right. It's hard enough living with Nuri, without landing him in trouble with you!'

'Oh, Laurette!' He said it softly and with a faint edge of despair on his voice, so that she hastily sipped her tea and tried not to look at him. She was not sure what lay behind that resigned, softly spoken reproach, and she was not sure she wanted to know at the moment.

She was a bit later arriving to see Ian than she expected, and Laurette found him waiting for her impatiently, though he did his best to disguise it when she finally did arrive. He looked so well that it was hard to believe that only three days ago he had looked so ill, and she found him in the hotel gardens on a seat shaded by a magnificent plane tree.

Like a huge green umbrella it spread above a flower bed massed with azaleas, roses and magnolias against a background of fluffy pink tamarisk, and the air that blew coolly across her forehead was scented and sweet.

Sitting down on the garden seat beside him, she let him take her hands in his, and he leaned across and kissed her mouth, with such an air of possessiveness that it gave her a few moments' uneasiness. Then sitting back he held her hands, while his blue eyes regarded her searchingly, noting the slight suggestion of spikiness on her lashes that betrayed those few tears she had shed earlier.

'Is something wrong, Laurette? What's been happening that I should know about?'

'Why, nothing, of course!'

'You've been crying.' He used the tip of one finger to stroke the spikey lashes. 'Why, Laurette?'

'Oh, I got a little bit worked up about something, that's all. I'm not always the level headed Scots lass, you know, Ian. Sometimes I get temperamental and the fur flies!' She laughed, determined to make little of it, but Ian still held both her hands and kept her facing him on the seat. 'I'm sorry I was late, Ian, but I'm here now.'

'Who made you late, Nuri Bey?'

She did not like the tone of his voice, but she preferred to change the subject rather than become involved in a discussion about Nuri. 'I'd rather not talk

125

about my family, Ian. Can't we find some other subject?'

It looked for a while as if he might insist, but then he shrugged suddenly and apparently relinquished the idea. An arm slid about her shoulders and he pulled her close until his cheek rested against hers. 'Then let's talk about us.' His voice was soft and whispered against her ear. 'I rather want to talk about you and me, lovely cousin, and you have to humour me while I'm a sick man, don't you?'

'You're not a sick man any longer, are you?' She managed to keep a lightness in her voice and steered him away from personal matters. In so many ways he was a stranger still, and she felt a certain detachment from him that she could not yet overcome. 'We'd better not go out anywhere, because you're not well enough for that yet, but we can walk around the gardens here and stay in the shade.'

He leaned towards her until his mouth was close to her ear once more and this time he pressed his lips to her soft skin, his face buried in the riot of soft silky hair. 'I have to decide what I'm going to do about you, sweetheart.'

She knew she became suddenly stiff in the circle of his arm, and he reacted by pulling her closer, pressing his mouth to the pulse that throbbed urgently and betrayed the anxious thudding of her heart. 'You don't have to decide what to do with me, Ian. Why should you?'

'Oh, but I think I do, my lovely.' He kissed her neck once more, smiling at her in a way that made her alarmingly uneasy. 'Didn't I tell you yet—I'm planning to take you home with me when I go?'

Her fingers dug into his arm as she pushed him away so that she could see his face, her eyes wide and

126

slightly vague, trying to tell herself she had not heard him right. 'I can't think what gives you that idea. Ian. You know I don't want to leave here.'

'Don't you want to go home?'

'But I *am* home!' He still didn't understand that, and she wondered if he ever would.

'Oh, Laurette—sweet little cousin! You're not Turkish, no matter how hard that black-eyed foster-brother of yours has tried to make you over. You're English, or Scottish, I don't care which you choose; but you're not Turkish and that's what concerns me! I want you away from here before you lose your identity any further. You're a Kearn, not a Kayaman, and I think you're in danger of forgetting that.'

Something in Laurette fought hard to resist, and yet her common sense told her that a good deal of what Ian said was true. She had become very Turkish during her time with her foster-family, but what Ian saw as a drawback, she saw as a comfort. Even in her more emotional exchanges with Nuri, there was a sense of belonging.

The sudden lurching coldness in her heart reminded her that it was during one of those exchanges that Nuri had suggested she would no longer belong at Yarev once Halet was married, and the reminder gave her that curiously lost feeling once more, that was so frightening. Unconsciously her fingers tightened over Ian's hand and he was looking at her curiously.

'Perhaps I could take a holiday somewhere—after Halet's married, there's a lot to do before then.'

'Be*fore* Halet's married, Laurette.' Ian's hand on her cheek turned her to look directly at him, and she saw how serious his blue eyes looked. 'I'll be flying back to England in another couple of weeks, and I've rather banked on you coming with me when I go.'

127

'Oh, but Ian, I can't!'

She made the denial hastily and with no pretence of considering it as a serious proposition, although obviously it was, judging by Ian's expression. The frantic beating of her heart was making her feel curiously lightheaded, and her brain simply refused to function clearly, for the idea of going back with him when he went home had not even occurred to her.

'You're turning it down flat—just like that?'

He sounded not only disappointed but angry, and she could imagine that somehow or other he would cast Nuri as the reason behind her refusal. She could hardly expect him to see it her way, of course, but somehow she wished it was easier to convince him that her foster-family were in no way the oppressors he saw them as.

'I couldn't leave just before Halet's wedding, Ian, you must see that.'

She sounded reasonable, she thought, and not in the least as if she condemned his reaction, but he was looking at her with a different look in his eyes—a hardness she had never seen there before, and it reminded her how little she knew him yet, even though he was her cousin.

'Are you involved in the wedding too?'

Obviously he disliked that idea as well, but she nodded, and a slight tilt to her chin defied him to find fault with her admission. 'Yes, of course I am, Halet's my sister.'

She half expected him to denounce that illusion too, but all he did was look at her and shake his head. 'And you don't give a damn about how I feel, do you, Laurette?'

It was a harsh and unfair verdict and she wished he had not made it. 'Ian, you know that isn't true, but——'

Her hands fluttered in a curiously helpless gesture as she tried to explain how she felt. 'You've known me for less than five days, so it can't really be so important to you whether or not I fly back to England with you.'

'It's important that you're my cousin, though not to you, apparently.'

'Your second cousin.' She made the correction automatically and knew in her heart that she was simply making excuses not to go with him. 'I've known Halet for most of my life, Ian, I can't—I won't stay away for the most important day of her life.'

His short hard fingers stroked absently at the soft skin of her upper arms and he looked much too despondent for a man who had simply been told by a virtual stranger that she would not go away with him. 'So that's it, then, is it? You won't fly home with me?'

'I'm sorry, Ian.'

She was genuinely sorry, she told herself, even though her life was due to suffer an upheaval anyway, even if she stayed. Somehow she could not face the idea of leaving altogether. Moving away from Yarev, perhaps to live with Latife and her husband was not the same thing as going right away, and plunging into a whole new world at the instigation of a man she scarcely knew, and perhaps never seeing her family again for years. No matter how categorically Ian declared her not part of the Kayaman family, in her heart she felt she was, and that was what mattered.

He was looking at her and using one finger to trace a pattern on the softness of her arm. 'You're a mouse, pretty cousin, do you realise that?' His smile, like his voice, had an edge of sharpness. 'You're safe in your warm little harem and you won't venture out, will you?'

Fearing there might just be a grain of truth in what he said, Laurette did not look at him, but shook her

129

head vaguely, and kept her lashes over the uncertainty in her eyes. 'You still don't understand, Ian, and I wish you did.'

'Understand?'

'How it is.' She used her hands again in that vaguely fluttering movement without realising how much it was like the form of silent communication used by the village women.

'Oh, I understand all right!' He leaned forward suddenly and kissed her mouth with a lingering warmth that made her close her eyes instinctively. 'But I've got another couple of weeks to do something about it,' he whispered against her ear. 'I'll think of some way of persuading you to my way of thinking.'

'I won't change my mind, Ian!'

'Maybe!' He smiled and his blue eyes had a determined gleam that reminded her discomfitingly of Nuri's in some curious way. 'But you will come with me to Alanya tomorrow, won't you?'

The invitation, coming so soon after more serious matters, took her momentarily by surprise, and she looked at him uncertainly, then remembered he planned for them to go somewhere each day. 'Isn't it a little soon, Ian? I mean, wouldn't it be wiser for you to wait a day or two before we go so far?'

From his expression it was clear he read some other motive into her reluctance, and he was shaking his head, a hint of smile giving his mouth a slightly bitter look. 'O.K.,' he said quietly, 'so we'll find a little beach somewhere nearby and swim. *Can* you swim?'

Sensing sarcasm, she flushed and lifted her chin, her eyes showing a warning glint that he took note of. 'Of course I can, Ian. My father taught me to swim as soon as I could walk almost.'

'Then we'll swim!'

She nodded, saying nothing about the need to buy a swim suit, for she had not swum for several years now, and did not possess one. Ian had enough reasons for thinking her a harem mouse without giving him further cause. 'We'll swim,' she echoed.

CHAPTER SEVEN

'IT is very daring, Laurette.' Halet was sitting on the bed in Laurette's room, her dark eyes passing judgment on the new swim suit bought especially for her outing with Ian, and her appraisal was hardly calculated to inspire confidence in the wearer. 'Will you not feel very—bold wearing such a costume?'

Laurette knew exactly what she meant as she eyed her reflection in a full-length mirror. The suit was French inspired and would have passed virtually unnoticed on any continental beach, but amid the rather exotic splendour of her bedroom it looked terribly out of place and much more revealing than she expected.

The trouble was that she had been in far too much of a hurry to give the purchase much thought and she had not stopped to try it on in the shop. Instead she had judged its appearance on the shop dummy that displayed it, making no allowances for the fact that an inanimate model bore little resemblance to the moving shape of a flesh and blood woman, nor did it have the same softly feminine curves.

'I have doubts,' she confessed after a second or two. 'But it's too late to change it now, Halet; and it really isn't too outrageous by present standards.'

'But by our standards?' Halet ventured, soft-voiced, and Laurette followed her meaning perfectly.

The suit was red and white and covered very little of her body. In fact it was very little more than two very small pieces of material and she was tempted to keep her arms crossed over her breast, although doing so gave her a curiously hunched appearance that Ian was sure to find amusing. She knew who she had in mind when she felt that curling sense of embarrassment, of course, and it was thinking of what Nuri would say if he ever saw it that made her react the way she did.

With one hand on her hip and her shoulders pulled back, she walked across the bedroom with a swaying gait that exaggerated a model girl's strut. Her chin dipped, she looked across at Halet with a bright, seductive smile on her face and fluttered her eyelashes.

'Oh, *hayir*, *hayir*, Laurette!' Halet looked at her in alarm, even though a glimmer of suppressed laughter showed in her dark eyes. 'If you behave so in that costume men will think you are——'

'You mean *Nuri* would think I was no better than I ought to be,' Laurette corrected her, and laughed a little wildly as she once more surveyed herself in the long mirror. 'He would get a bit of a shock, wouldn't he? Though most men these days wouldn't turn a hair.'

'Will not your cousin, Ian, also be shocked?' Halet enquired innocently, and Laurette smiled at her reflected image musingly.

'Actually their reactions probably wouldn't be all that different—but Ian would be more honest about it.'

As if she feared it might be put to the test, Halet regarded her anxiously. 'You will not let Nuri see you?'

Shaking her head as she pulled her dress on over the bikini, Laurette laughed. 'Not if I can help it! Knowing Nuri he'd probably have me confined to my room for the rest of the week!'

'He would not like it,' Halet affirmed, and Laurette thought that in her quiet way she was almost as much a

133

goad to her conscience as N··ri was.

She smoothed her hanus down over the dress that now concealed the controversial swim suit and sighed. 'Oh well, with a bit of luck he'll never know anything about it. Now I'd better go before Ian comes hammering on the door demanding to know where I am.'

Laurette had little idea where they were, except that they had turned off the main highway when Ian spotted what he decided was an ideal place for them to bathe from. There were any number of little sandy beaches along this coast and some of them, like this one, were completely deserted.

She had no complaint about his choice, for it was quite idyllic and offered everything one could ask of a bathing beach. Trees grew right down to the water's edge and gave the romantic illusion of a desert island as well as giving shade from the sun, and the land curved gently to form a shallow bay so that they seemed to be in a small world of their own.

To add to the air of romanticism, right at the tip of one curve of the bay a ruined castle stood outlined against the bright blue sky, its ragged walls running right down into the sea, like the broken teeth of a giant animal. A stark reminder of the past that was never very far away in Turkey, and even beautiful in its own way, though possibly dangerous to the incautious.

There were natural rocks in plenty too, thrusting up through the sand, ideal places for use as changing rooms, although in fact Ian laughed at the idea of the necessity of using them when they both had their costumes on under their clothes.

Laurette rather self-consciously pulled off her dress and looked down at the new red and white bikini with even more misgivings. It looked every bit as provocative here on this small deserted beach as it had at home in her bedroom, and already she sensed Ian was taking an interest in it.

It had seldom before struck her how much lighter-skinned he was than Nuri and her foster-father, and she noticed it now with some surprise as he stood stripped down to a pair of dark trunks. Of course he was new to sunny climes and his skin less accustomed to the hot sun, hence his vulnerability to sunstroke on their last outing. But somehow it seemed to make him even more of a stranger to her and that was oddly discomfiting in the present situation.

He made no attempt to conceal his approval of the red and white swim suit and, although she anticipated it, it nevertheless gave her a curious sense of shyness to be so openly admired. 'You look terrific, cousin!' He took her hands and drew her towards him, but she resisted and that obviously surprised him. It showed in his blue eyes and the suggestion of tightness about his lips. 'I won't eat you, love, though you look good enough to eat!'

Her defensiveness was an instinct, born of those endless exchanges with Nuri, and she looked at him with bright blue eyes and a flush on her cheeks. 'I'm not objecting, Ian, but I——'

'You're not used to wearing a bikini!' He laughed softly, as if the realisation amused him, and he was shaking his head. Still holding her hands, he swept his gaze over her flushed face until it came to rest on her mouth, then he smiled. 'You should wear one more often, Laurette, get used to the feeling of freedom. You're certainly worth looking at in that scrap of nothing.'

'I feel—brassy.'

She admitted it defensively, and Ian laughed, shaking his head to deny it. 'Not you, cousin! I'll admit you're a definite temptation in that bikini, but then you're a temptation done up to the neck in a nice modest little dress—you're just that sort of a girl!'

Her heart was beating anxiously fast and she felt strangely isolated suddenly, and rather alarmingly excited, a combination she neither understood nor trusted. There was an earthy quality about Ian that she had never noticed quite so much before, and he held her hands tightly, almost as if he suspected she might turn away and run.

His copper-bright head gleamed in the hot sun above those blue eyes that so often reminded her of her father's, and yet now looked nothing like him. Holding her at arms' length for a second, he sent a swift and unmistakably appreciative gaze over her slim rounded figure, then he leaned forward suddenly and lightly kissed her mouth.

'O.K., let's swim and relax a little, shall we? That's what we're here for.'

With Ian pulling her by the hand, she went down the sandy beach after him, and she had to admit that she had never enjoyed the water more. It seemed such a long time since she had done any swimming, but she found she had lost none of her skill, and she gave Ian a lively time trying to keep up with her as she dived and swam in the soft blue ocean.

He was quite a strong swimmer, but she was quick and lithe as a seal in the warm waters of the Mediterranean, and for the most part she managed to evade his attempts to catch her. 'You're too fast for me!' He made the admission in a voice flattened by distance and the density of water, shaking back his red hair that now looked much more dark. A stroke or two brought him closer, and his teeth gleamed in a smile as he came within reach. 'You're as evasive as a mermaid, cousin; give me a chance, will you?'

Going with the tide, they had drifted nearer to the ruined castle on the further side of their little bay, but it still appeared only as a starkly ragged outline against the blue sky, and she scarcely paid it heed as she laughed at his plea.

Glancing back briefly to see if he was likely to be quick enough to catch her this time, she dived down into the warm blue water once more, her head turned, looking for Ian. She could see nothing of him beyond a slight disturbance in the blue water in her wake as he dived down in pursuit of her, and it was the last thing she remembered for quite a while. She turned back only a fraction of a second before her head came into contact with the hidden bastions of the old castle below the surface of the water.

For quite some time nothing meant anything more than a jumble of sounds and vague sensations, and when Laurette eventually opened her eyes it was to see a friendly but completely strange face bending over her. A Turkish face, she had no doubt, but obviously a woman of authority, and wearing a white overall coat. A stethoscope, only half concealed in a pocket, gave a further clue, and Laurette frowned at her curiously.

'Are you feeling better?'

A standard question the world over, but Laurette took a moment to gather her wits, and the tip of her tongue flicked hastily over dry lips as she coped for a moment with a curious sense of unreality.

'I—I think so, thank you.'

'That's good!' A cool, efficient hand rolled back one eyelid and a torch was shone into the pupil dazzling her for a moment before the process was repeated with the other eye. Evidently the examination was satisfactory, for the examiner nodded and repeated her verdict. 'Good, good!'

Laurette looked around her at the small, clinically neat room, and came to the obvious conclusion. 'This is a hospital?'

'This is the Lemiz Clinic, and I am Doctor Alcilic, Miss Kearn.' A brief warm smile crossed the smooth face and only just failed to disguise the curiosity that lurked in the dark eyes. 'You have had a very lucky escape.'

Laurette thought very carefully for a second. Her heart was thudding hard and she felt strangely light-headed, but she could not think how she came to be in a hospital bed. Her head hurt and she suspected it was bandaged, though she had not so far used her hands to confirm it.

She surely should be able to remember how she had been hurt, but somehow she could not, and the sense of helplessness that gave her brought panic flooding in its wake, so that she looked at the doctor with eyes that showed the stark, blank look of fear.

'I—I don't know what happened to me!' Her voice too echoed the way she felt, and the doctor's cool, matter-of-fact assurance did nothing to relieve the feeling. 'I can't remember—I can't remember anything about it!'

'That is perfectly natural, Miss Kearn. There is no cause for alarm at all—believe me that it will come back to you in the normal course of things. You must rest and remain quiet, that is all. The head wound is small and no cause for concern, but you have to rest.'

'Head wound?' Laurette reached up and gingerly felt the patch of adhesive plaster that seemed to cover

138

half her forehead. A small wound it might be, but it throbbed violently, and made her feel slightly sick. 'I —I hit my head?'

'On a submerged wall, apparently. I have heard only the outline of the story, my main concern was to treat you.' The doctor straightened up, her smile confident and professional. 'If you feel able to see a visitor, there is someone to see you. Do you feel well enough?'

She expected it to be Ian, though she was not quite sure why, but whoever it was Laurette would be glad to see someone she knew. Her confidence was in need of support and she felt alarmingly vague about everything. 'I want to see someone, please, doctor. I—I want to see my family.'

Kindly but businesslike, the doctor smiled. 'You will have to make do with Madame Ocak for the moment, I am afraid—she is here and waiting to see you.'

'Latife?' Relief enveloped Laurette, bringing her close to tears. She needed someone like Latife at the moment. The eldest Kayaman daughter was very much like her mother had been, with the same gentle and motherly manner towards her young foster-sister, and she could have wished for no one better. 'Oh, please let me see her!'

The white coat moved silently to the door, and a moment later the dark, pretty face of Latife Ocak peeped round at her, a smile on her face that did not quite reach her eyes. '*Bebek!*' A light kiss brushed her aching brow and Latife's exotic perfume enveloped her for a second or two when she bent over her. Clucking sympathetically, Latife sat beside her bed holding her hand consolingly. 'How is your poor head, *bebek*, hmm?'

'It aches!' Touching the plaster gingerly, Laurette tried a laugh that did not quite come off, but sounded instead as if she was about to burst into tears. 'I—I don't know what happened to me, Latife; I can't remember anything about it.'

'Suna has told me, but she also says that there is nothing to worry about, that it will come back to you before very long.'

'Suna?'

Latife smiled. 'Suna Alcilic. You met her at the party the other night, do you not remember? The same party at which you met your cousin, Ian. Her husband is a business acquaintance of Furedin's.'

'I don't remember.'

It was obvious that nothing was of any real interest to Laurette at the moment except the puzzle of her own situation, and Latife squeezed her hand reassuringly. 'I have spoken to Suna, Laurette, and she is quite adamant that the loss of remembrance is temporary. You must not concern yourself with what happened at the moment, only with getting well.'

'Yes. Yes, I suppose so.'

It must be reaction, of course, but she felt horribly tearful and there was nothing she could do about the fat rolling tears that coursed down her cheeks. Latife was on her feet in a moment, bending over her, anxious and solicitous.

'Oh, Laurette *bebek*, please do not cry. You will soon feel well again, I can promise you.'

'I'm—I'm sorry.' She bit her lips, but the tears continued to roll dismally down her cheeks, and Latife gently dabbed them away with her handkerchief. 'I don't even remember where I was when I was hurt, or even if I was with Ian. I think I was, but I can't be sure.'

'You were, *bebek*.'

She answered promptly but so quietly that something in her voice struck a response in Laurette's chaotic brain. 'Is he all right? Was he hurt too?' She clutched her aching head and closed her eyes in another desperate attempt to remember. 'Oh, I wish I could remember!'

'You will, *bebek*, you will.' Latife's cool hand smoothed the hair back from her brow and once more the perfume she knew so well enveloped her. 'It was your cousin who called Baba and told him what had happened.' A small, rueful smile touched her mouth for a moment as if she recognised Ian's feelings too. 'I think he was a little frightened and needed someone to share his fear, poor man.'

'Baba Refik has been told?' There was something in the back of her mind that kept evading her. Something to do with Baba Refik, or Nuri, or perhaps both of them, but she simply could not remember what it was.

Latife nodded, but there was a hint of curiosity in her eyes for a second, as if she suspected there was something on her mind. 'Your cousin did right to let us know, of course, *bebek*, but if he had not Suna Alcilic would have contacted us as a matter of course. We are still your recognised family, even though you now have this new cousin.'

Resentment was a new side to Latife's character, and Laurette recognised it with some surprise, even though she was so preoccupied with trying to recall what it was she did not want her foster-father to know about. 'Baba Refik is here?'

'One visitor only is allowed at the present time, and it was considered that I was best suited to be the one.' Her dark eyes had a briefly speculative look, half concealed by thick black lashes. 'Nuri brought me here in his car. He is waiting outside to learn how you are.'

Nuri—it seemed inevitable somehow that he should have come, but hearing his name only brought that

141

curiously elusive problem to the front of her mind again. 'There was something——' She pressed her hand to her aching head once more and frowned. 'I can't remember what it was, Latife, but there was something—something to do with Nuri—or Baba Refik—I can't remember——'

'Did they know that you were going swimming with your cousin Ian, Laurette?'

'Swimming?'

Once again something triggered in her mind, but still refused to be identified, and she frowned over it painfully, so that Latife reached out and touched her hand. 'You do not remember that?' If she did it was only vaguely, and Latife went on, her soft voice gently probing her memory. 'It was in a little bay just a short distance off the Alanya road. Your cousin got help from someone passing and an ambulance was sent for you.'

A whole gamut of half remembered sensation whirled through Laurette's aching head, but still no clear picture emerged, and from the expression on Latife's face it was obvious that she expected a response of some kind. Swimming in a small bay with Ian; it should mean something, but at the moment it only meant a jumble of senseless half-remembered sights and sounds.

'I think I remember going for a swim, Latife, but I can't—I can't quite——'

'Then better to leave it, *bebek*.' A soft hand smoothed her brow and she closed her eyes to enjoy the comfort of its touch. 'It is enough that you are safe and no worse harm has come to you. We were all very concerned.'

Laurette remembered Nuri waiting outside to learn how she was, and she opened her eyes again a sudden thrill of anticipation stirring in her stomach as

142

she looked at Latife through the thickness of her lashes. 'Is—is Nuri coming in to see me?'

'No, *bebek*.' Her voice was gentle, understanding, and somehow it seemed she was apologising. 'Only one visitor was allowed; he came only to drive me and to assure himself that all was well with you. He will not be coming in to see you.'

'He's angry?'

It seemed inevitable somehow, though she had no idea what was likely to have caused it in this particular instance, and she knew she was at least partly right when Latife did not deny it outright. Instead her hand was patted gently and a gentle smile sought to reassure her.

'He is—disturbed, *bebek*, and worried that you are hurt.'

It was useless to try and stop the tears that flowed, but Laurette brushed them away impatiently with the back of her hand. 'It isn't fair of him to be angry when I don't know what I've done! I want to know what happened and then I can tell him—oh please, Latife, can't you tell me what happened? Didn't Ian tell you?'

'Only that you hit your head on a submerged wall while you were swimming. He is a little vague, you will understand, and he was not very close when it happened. So much blood frightened him badly and he was concerned only with your well-being.'

A shiver ran through her suddenly, perhaps induced by a sudden recollection of a dark looming blackness in the water immediately ahead of her and then—nothing. 'How long will I have to stay in here, Latife?'

'Not for very long, *bebek*, Suna has promised that. But you must rest until she says you are well enough to come home.'

'I'll be allowed other visitors?'

Latife's dark eyes cast swiftly over her pale face, and she half smiled. 'You refer to your cousin?' She did not wait for an answer but got to her feet again and stood looking down at her for a moment. 'I am sure it will be allowed, perhaps tomorrow, if you ask Doctor Alcilic.'

'Do you have to go now?'

Laurette felt far too much as if she was being deserted, and yet it made sense that she should be kept quiet and did not see too many people at first. Latife bent and kissed her forehead gently. 'I will come again tomorrow, *bebek*. Now I must return and tell them all how much better you are than we expected—it will be a great relief to them.'

Laurette thought of Nuri waiting outside, and she tried to understand the irrepressible need she felt to see him. It made no sort of sense, especially since she was almost sure he was angry about her accident, yet she wanted to see him so much that she almost mentioned it to Latife, only drawing back at the last minute.

Instead she raised herself in the bed slightly when Latife opened the door to go, and looked beyond her into the corridor. Meeting with only a blank, cream-painted wall but no sign of Nuri, she sank back against the pillows with an overwhelming sense of disappointment and turned her face away. Perhaps he would come tomorrow.

Doctor Alcilic was willing enough to allow as many visitors as she liked the following day, and she seemed more than satisfied with the progress she was making. 'There is a young man to see you,' she told Laurette as she pushed her pen back into the pocket of her overall coat, and once more that barely disguised glimpse of curiosity puzzled her. 'I shall let him come in, hmm?'

Laurette's heart was hammering at her ribs with

144

quite unaccountable force and she instinctively put up a hand to smooth her hair when the smiling doctor walked across to the door. 'Oh yes, please let him come in!'

'Your visitor.' The dark eyes looked back at her and the hint of smile on her mouth said a great deal more than her simple announcement did. 'Do not tire her by staying too long, please!'

The warning was given as the visitor passed her in the doorway and heaven knew why she expected Nuri, but a second after Ian walked into the room Laurette felt a sense of disappointment. Just as she had yesterday when she failed to catch a glimpse of Nuri in the corridor.

Holding out his hands to her, Ian ignored the chair beside the bed and sat instead on the edge of the bed itself, his blue eyes searching her face and coming to rest on the disfiguring plaster across her brow, its top edge covered by copper-bright hair. For the moment he looked more serious than she ever remembered before.

'Laurette! Are you all right?'

'I'm fine now, Ian, apart from an aching head, and even that's much better than it was yesterday.'

'I couldn't get in to see you yesterday.' It was obvious the situation had not pleased him. 'It was one visitor only, and it seemed to be agreed that Madame Ocak should be the one.'

'You got the ambulance and got me in here, though, Ian, so I'm told, and the family are very grateful to you—so am I.'

Ian's blue eyes regarded her steadily for a second. 'I'm family, love, remember?'

'Oh yes—I'm sorry; but you know what I mean.'

He nodded, prepared not to argue the point for the

145

moment. 'They tell me you've lost your memory, is that right?'

It sounded rather too dramatic put like that, though she supposed it was true. Since Latife had told her as much as she could yesterday she had had time to dwell on it, and she thought things were a little clearer this morning.

'It isn't nearly as bad as it sounds, Ian. I've just— gone a little muzzy about the actual accident, that's all, but Doctor Alcilic says it will come back in time.'

'That's your lady doctor?' She nodded, sensing something in his manner. 'A friend of the family, I understand?'

'Her husband and Furedin are business acquaintances. Latife says I've met her before, at the same party where I met you, but I don't remember her.'

'I do. I recognised her when I brought you in yesterday, and she knew me too, though I don't think she realised where from. She knew you, though, and I could see her trying to figure out how come you were with me.' His eyes were bright and glittering like gems in his sunburned face and his fingers tightened around hers as he looked at her. 'Good God, Laurette, they've even got someone to keep an eye on you in here!'

'Ian!' She looked at him in dismay. His visit was welcome, but not if he had come simply to complain about her family, as he so often did. 'It's just a co-incidence that Doctor Alcilic knows Latife and Furedin, if she's involved in her husband's social life, she was bound to know them.'

'And it's just a happy coincidence that she happens to be in charge of your case!'

'Yes!' Her head was beginning to ache again and she knew it would not take too much to make her weepy again, as she had been yesterday. 'Ian, I—I——'

As if he realised suddenly, Ian took her hands again and held them tightly, his face anxious as he leaned across to kiss her mouth. 'I'm sorry, my sweet, I'm rather shaken by all this. There was so much blood, you looked as if—my God, I actually thought you were dead at first, and I didn't know what on earth to do for the best.' He looked down at their clasped hands, and his bowed head had a curiously tense look about it that puzzled her. 'I—I almost ran off and left you, Laurette, I was so damned scared!'

'Oh, Ian!'

She did not want to believe it, but she had never been in a position like that and she could not judge what her reaction was likely to be. He was shaking his head, still not looking at her, and his voice was strangely flat, as if he said what he did after much consideration.

'I thought about your family, what they would say, whether they'd think twice about accusing me—oh, I know it sounds ridiculous now, but I kept thinking about Nuri Kayaman and I was *scared*!' He looked up at last and a faint, rueful smile tugged at the corners of his good-humoured mouth. 'Good job for me that the Kearns are a sensible breed on the whole and not really cowardly. Somehow I got you on to the beach out of the sun and went to find help.'

'You did wonderfully well in the circumstances.'

Ian smiled wryly. 'Yeah! I wasn't exactly dressed for hitch-hiking and it wasn't until I got back that I thought about putting my clothes on again. Luckily a car came along and the driver turned up trumps. You were in here in a remarkably quick time.'

The last few words fell on partially deaf ears, for Laurette was thinking back. Something he had said distracted her and it took her a moment or two to realise what it was. The something that she had been so

147

anxious about concerning Nuri and Baba Refik—she thought she knew now what it was and she looked at Ian curiously, ignoring the ache in her head.

'Ian, when I was brought in here, what was I wearing?'

He smiled and winked an eye at her, his brows flicking upwards in unmistakable meaning. 'Why, that itsybitsy bikini, of course, love. Your dress got left behind on the beach, I'm afraid, I just never gave it another thought, and your bag was already in the car.'

'Oh!'

She could all too easily imagine what the reaction would be at home when they learned she had been brought into the clinic wearing nothing but that tiny scrap of a swimsuit she had been rash enough to buy and wear—the one she had hoped neither Nuri nor her foster-father would ever see.

At the moment she was wearing a white hospital gown, but she had no doubt that her swimsuit had been put safely to one side until she was ready to leave, and Doctor Alcilic would have made a note of how scantily she had been dressed, although she was probably too discreet to say anything.

Ian was watching her, still holding her hands and his eyes searched her face with mingled anxiety and curiosity. 'What's wrong, Laurette?'

It would be difficult to tell him without raising the old controversies, but he was expecting some kind of an answer, so she made it as light as she could manage in the circumstances. 'I'm just thinking that it must have given some of them a shock to see me in that swimsuit!'

His eyes narrowed, he scanned her face for a moment, noting the faint flush in her cheeks. 'So *that's* it!' He gripped her hands in his tightly enough to hurt and made her look at him. 'Laurette, you can wear just

148

whatever you like, do you hear me? You don't have to have their approval before you wear a bikini—you'd never get it anyway!'

'I didn't say——'

'You didn't have to!' Ian interrupted harshly. 'I can just imagine Nuri Bey looking down that long nose of his at you daring to wear anything like that, but it's none of his damned business, and you tell him so if he raises the matter!'

'Ian, please don't shout, my head hurts.'

'I'm sorry, love!' He was contrite, reaching to draw her into his arms, when there was a knock on the door, and he cursed under his breath as he drew back, his hands still on her arms. 'What the——'

'There is another visitor for you, *hanim*.' A young nurse blushed to the roots of her hair at the scene she imagined she had interrupted, and blinked uncertainly for a moment. 'If it is——'

'Oh no, no, please show him—her in!'

Instinctively, yet again, Laurette's mind had picked on Nuri as her visitor, but it was no real surprise when Halet walked in instead, in fact she breathed an inward sigh of relief. Maybe she was as much aware that Ian had been about to kiss her, but she would make far less fuss about it.

'Halet! Oh, I'm glad to see you!'

Halet smiled, her dark eyes fluttering in the direction of Ian's disgruntled face for a second only. 'I am not an inconvenient visitor?'

What Ian would have told her, Laurette had no idea, but she hastily made her own decision. 'No, of course you're not; you can have the chair since Ian's not using it.'

Clearly Halet had something on her mind, and Laurette knew her well enough to recognise it. 'I came to—I came to bring you some other clothes.' The meaning in her dark eyes was unmistakable, and Laurette felt like hugging her. Sweet, understanding Halet, knowing she did not want the menfolk to find out about that daring swimsuit, had somehow managed to get herself elected the one to bring her some clothes.

'Oh, Halet, thank you!' Laurette reached up her arms and hugged her, while Ian worked it out for himself, his frown clearly showing that he too followed her meaning, and liked it a lot less.

He sat on the edge of her bed, with Laurette's hands in his once more, and squeezed her fingers hard. 'You have it all nicely settled between you, don't you?' he said, his voice flat and resigned. 'You never intended them to find out about that bikini?'

Leaning back against the pillows, Laurette smiled at Halet. 'Not if we could help it,' she agreed.

CHAPTER EIGHT

IT had not been easy to convince Ian that by far the best plan was for her foster-father and Halet to fetch her home from the clinic, but Laurette had eventually persuaded him. He was determined to establish himself firmly as her cousin, she realised, and took every possible opportunity to remind her of the fact.

It seemed strange that she could feel so out of touch after only a couple of days in hospital, but she had a curious sense of unreality when she walked out into the sunshine again, that she could not understand at all. She felt disturbingly unsure of everything, although her foster-father's genuinely warm welcome did a lot to restore her confidence.

Halet was unmistakably delighted to have her home again, and she chattered endlessly in the car coming back, so that she earned a soft cluck of reproach from her father and subsided, verbally at least. She still glanced repeatedly over her shoulder at Laurette and her bright dark eyes left her pleasure in no doubt at all.

It was good to be at home, and the sight of Yarev behind its secret walls and lush gardens touched Laurette so deeply that she wondered how much harder it was going to be to leave it for good when Halet married. With the sweet familiar scents surrounding her she walked along the path to the house with Refik Kayaman on one side of her and Halet on the other, and the tall slim cypress that stood guard by the iron gate cast its long morning shadow the whole length of the wall. It was all so quiet and peaceful, so familiar and so secure.

Across the hall, as they went into the house, the door of the *salon* stood partly open, and it was instinctive to glance across at it, half expecting to see Nuri come out to welcome her. But of course he didn't. He would be at the office at this hour of the day, with much more important things to think about.

Sensitive to her train of thought to a disconcerting degree, her foster-father followed the direction of her glance, and smiled in understanding. 'Nuri is not yet home, *bebek*, he will welcome you when he comes!' A house servant hovering on the far side of the hall caught the old man's eye, and he nodded, turning to Laurette again when the silent instruction was apparently understood. 'We will have *çay*, *bebek*, eh? I am sure you will welcome some.'

'Oh yes, please, lovely!' She walked across the hall with him, and Halet only half a step behind them, and she was suddenly so overwhelmed by the love she had for her adopted family that she impulsively pushed her arm through Refik Kayaman's as she had once done with Nuri, and hugged him. 'Oh, Baba Refik, I'm so *glad* to be home!'

If the old man was surprised by her emotion he did not show it, but smiled to himself when she settled on the ottoman beside him, while Halet sat close by in one of the armchairs. 'You must tell us about this accident, how it happened. We understand from Doctor Alcilic that you have now recovered your memory.'

'Yes, mostly I have.' She was choosing her words carefully, conscious of doing so, yet unsure why she was doing it. 'I remember going in the water, then swimming, diving and larking about with Ian, but I don't really remember hitting my head.'

152

If Refik Kayaman questioned the meaning of larking about he gave no indication. His smile was as blandly understanding as ever, and he gave her his whole attention. 'You swim well, of course, I remember how skilled you were as a child.'

'Daddy taught me early on. He couldn't always keep an eye on me and we were very near the sea, he thought it safer.'

'He was a wise man,' Refik Kayaman observed quietly, 'and a much loved one.' The dark eyes looked at her with gentle enquiry for a moment. 'Do you remember him well, Laurette?'

It was a question Laurette found hard to answer with any degree of certainty, for lately she had never been quite sure. The remembered face of her father, a face she had thought she would never forget, had become more and more overlaid by Ian's so similar features recently, until she was no longer sure which were common to both of them. Hugging her knees, she considered for a moment longer.

'I don't honestly know, Baba Refik. I feel sure I do sometimes, but then quite often lately, I'm not sure whether the face I picture is Daddy's or Ian's.'

'Your cousin is so much like my old friend?'

'He's very like him.' It surprised her to realise suddenly that Ian and her foster-father had never met. 'But of course you've never met Ian, have you?'

'Whenever he has called here for you I seem to have been occupied elsewhere and I have never had the pleasure of meeting him. It is an omission I very much regret.'

Laurette mused for a moment longer on the confusing similarities between Ian and her dead father. Perhaps Refik Kayaman would be a better judge of just how strong the similarities were, for he would see both men from the view of an adult.

'I'm sure you'd agree with me how alike they are, Baba Refik. Especially in certain things, like the colour of his hair, of course, and his eyes, but not only that. The way he holds his head, and a way of saying things, even the way he laughs.'

'Your father was a man who laughed a great deal.' He spoke softly, remembering his old friend's boisterous good humour, and he reached out and lightly touched her cheek for a moment. 'And naturally this strong likeness to your father draws you to him.'

'Well—yes, I suppose so.'

She was not sure just what was behind that rather enigmatic remark, and she looked at him for a second uncertainly. It was so difficult to know what was going on behind those dark, unfathomable eyes, for like Nuri, he could show a face that completely disguised whatever was going on in his mind.

'But it isn't *only* because he's like Daddy that I like Ian, Baba Refik. He's a very attractive man in his own right.'

Impulsively she looked to Halet to confirm it, then as hastily had second thoughts. Halet's eyes were downcast—no matter if she thought Ian an attractive man, she was unlikely to say so in her father's hearing.

'I'm sure you'd like him if you met him,' Laurette insisted, and her foster-father smiled.

'Perhaps it is time that we met, eh?'

She should have grasped the opportunity eagerly, Laurette told herself, but somehow she doubted if the meeting would be quite what Refik Kayaman envisaged. Something in the old man's voice too, made her uneasy. Perhaps she was ultra-sensitive at the moment, but she felt sure she detected some inflection in his

154

voice when he suggested it, as if something more than simple hospitality prompted it.

'Perhaps Mr Kearn would accept an invitation to dine with us one evening,' he went on when she did not reply. 'A few friends, just a small dinner party. We have not entertained for some time now, it would be pleasant to do so again and I will have the opportunity of meeting your cousin and judging for myself how like my old friend he is.'

'Of course, Baba Refik.'

Her own voice too betrayed her, she thought, for the old man was looking at her questioningly. 'Does the idea please you, Laurette? If you would prefer to wait until you are perhaps feeling more recovered——'

'No, no, I'm perfectly well again now.'

'Good, then we shall arrange it very soon, I think.'

'Ian goes back to England in about two weeks' time, he——' She bit back the words hastily. This wasn't the moment to say that Ian wanted to take her back with him, even though she had no intention of going with him. Hastily avoiding Halet's unexpectedly discerning glance, she hurried on, 'I'm sure he'd love to come, Baba.'

Perhaps Refik Kayaman had some inkling of the truth himself, but he was better at concealing his feelings than his daughter was, and even if he thought there was a likelihood of Ian persuading her to go with him, he would not simply charge her with the idea, but approach it with subtlety.

'Then we must make it soon, *bebek*, eh?' Laurette nodded silently, wondering if Ian would even accept the invitation, feeling as he did. 'And perhaps we may leave the matter of the invitation to you?'

'Yes, of course, Baba Refik.'

'I feel sure he will not refuse you,' he said, and smiled at her.

Laurette saw nothing of Nuri until the evening when he came back from the office as he did every other day. He had lunched with a business colleague, but that was not unusual enough to cause comment, it was simply that she felt his absence was in some way hurtful. It was unreasonable of her, of course, but she would have liked to think he took the trouble to come home and see how she was, her first day out of hospital.

She was alone in the *salon* when she heard him come in, and nothing she could do affected the sudden urgent beating of her heart when she heard his footsteps crossing the tiled floor in the hall, trying to judge whether or not he was coming in her direction. She was curled up on the ottoman, as usual, and the lamps were already lit, casting a soft golden glow over the exotically furnished room, and gleaming like flame on her copper-red head.

The door opened and with it half a dozen reflections of the same moment in the mirrors that hung on the walls, and she looked up quickly, her face shadowed and the expression in her eyes hidden for the moment by a dark fringe of lashes. One hand held the magazine she had been reading and the other lay flat-palmed on the fat cushions beside her.

'Hello, Nuri.'

Why that slightly defensive edge on her voice? she wondered. Why did she always suspect that he was going to either scold or criticise? There was no clue at all to his intention or his mood at the moment, and his face was simply a chiselled bronze mask in the yellow light. Only the black eyes glittered with life as he looked down at her.

'I was not able to come earlier, there was a—crisis that needed my attention.'

The almost-apology took her by surprise and it showed in her eyes. 'Oh, of course, I know you're busy.'

'Are you better?'

It all sounded so very formal that she almost laughed; instead she inclined her head and smiled. 'I'm perfectly all right now, apart from a sore head, thank you.' She touched the plaster that still decorated her brow and made a grimace of mock pain. 'It's not nearly as bad as this makes it look.'

'And your memory is recovered?'

'More or less. I'm still a bit muzzy, but I can remember most of what happened.' If only he would sit down instead of standing over her the way he was! She looked up and smiled invitingly, indicating a place on the ottoman beside her. 'I wish you'd sit down, you look so far away up there.'

Without a word he sat quite close beside her with his hands clasped between his knees. As he turned suddenly, the black eyes glowed like polished jet between those incredibly thick lashes scanning her face in a swift, explicit scrutiny that brought a flush to her cheeks and fluttered her heartbeat anxiously.

'What did happen, Laurette?'

'We went swimming.'

A slight frown drew at his black brows as if he disliked the idea of that. 'So I understand, but what happend when you were injured?'

'It was just sheer carelessness, I suppose.' She tried to make it sound far less serious than he obviously took it for, and somehow she had the feeling that he was trying to find some way of casting Ian as villain, something she had no intention of allowing. 'I should have looked where I was going and I didn't, it was as simple as that

157

really. We were swimming close to a ruined castle and some of the walls were under the water—I just didn't realise how close I was.'

'I see.'

It was rash, but it was also inevitable, and she looked up at him suddenly, a sparkle in her blue eyes that he had no difficulty in recognising. 'There's no possible way you can make it Ian's fault, Nuri, no way at all.'

If he had been angry she could hardly have been surprised, although she already regretted her outburst, as she so often did when it was too late. But instead he was looking at her steadily from only a hand's touch away, and there was even a small shadow of a smile on his firm straight mouth.

'I know you too well, *bebek*, to think you incapable of doing something as foolish as swimming around submerged ruins. I have no doubt at all that the fault was yours.' The smile became more evident and the black eyes challenging. 'Does that make you happier? To know that I do not blame your cousin for your accident?'

He had neatly turned the tables on her in a way she had not anticipated, and her mouth was reproachful as she looked at him for a moment in silence. 'At least Ian came and saw me in hospital,' she told him. '*You* didn't!'

'Did you wish me to?'

Taken unawares again, she blinked at him uneasily. It was all too easy remembering how anxiously she had looked for a visit from him, and how disappointed she had been when he did not come, but she was not going to tell him so. Not face to face like this with those black eyes watching her, as if he could guess the answer without her confirmation.

'I would have been glad to see you.' It was a compromise, and from his expression she thought it was more than he expected. 'I felt horribly—cut off from everybody while I was in there. I'd never been in hospital before.'

He reached out and touched the plaster on her forehead with a big, gentle hand that sent a flutter of sensation through her when she least expected it. 'Poor *bebek*.' His voice flowed, deep and soft, soothing as the hand on her brow, and she hastily lowered her eyes. 'We thought we had lost you when your cousin telephoned. He was so panic-stricken that he gave the impression you were—He spoke of so much blood from your head; that you were unconscious and in hospital.'

'It frightened him, he told me so.'

Nuri nodded, his face gentled by the soft lighting and his voice still had that soothing, deep sound that was so very affecting. 'It was frightening, little one. I cannot remember being so frightened since Ana died.'

It was more than she expected, this fear he spoke of, for she remembered just how stricken he had been when his mother died so suddenly and unexpectedly. She had known they would be worried, but she had not thought of them being so fearful for her, and especially not Nuri, so that she looked at him for a moment with wide, incredulous eyes, her lips parted in surprise.

'I—I didn't realise.'

Her own voice was soft and husky with emotion, not quite steady, a condition that Nuri's gentle hand on her brow did nothing to help. 'You did not realise how concerned we were for you? But surely you know by now how much you are one of us, *bebek*.'

'Ian said he was afraid, but I hadn't thought——'

'You think us less sensitive?' The tone of his voice was reproach enough, and she preferred not to meet his eyes. 'But how could you think that, Laurette, when we

159

have known you for so many years, and he is—a stranger to you?'

'Nuri——'

'He *is* a stranger, Laurette!' He was holding her hand in his, although she had not been aware of it happening, and from the way his strong fingers gripped her, she knew just how deeply he felt. 'How long have you known him?'

'Almost ten days.' She made the response automatically. 'But he *is* my cousin, Nuri. I—I suppose that makes a difference to the way he feels.'

'The way he feels! How is that, hmm? He tries to make you rebel against our ways——'

'Nuri, you can't blame Ian for making me into a rebel—you've always thought of me as one!'

'A tender rebel, perhaps, but not someone who deliberately sets out to deceive her family. This was never you until that man came here!'

'You don't like him!'

'I do not like him!' Hearing him confirm it in that flat, cool voice startled her for a moment, and a breath of a shiver fluttered along her back. 'I wish you were not so easily influenced by him, Laurette.'

It was hard to deny it because she knew that a good deal of what he said was true. Ian was determined to make her throw off the influence of her adopted family if he could, and somehow she could never quite bring herself to deny him the right to do so as firmly as she should.

'You—you make it sound as if I have no will of my own, and you of all people know that isn't true, Nuri.' Her hands tightly rolled in her lap, she was aware of him watching her, with that disturbing black-eyed scrutiny she was by now so accustomed to. 'Nuri'— she bit her lower lip anxiously, 'I—I wish we didn't always fight. I don't want to fight with you but some-how I always seem to, and——'

On the brink of tears, her eyes glistened as she looked up at him, and quite unexpectedly he was smiling. Just a hint of a smile at the corners of his mouth as he stretched out a hand and lightly touched her cheek with a finger-tip.

'Perhaps we are both too quick to anger, little one, eh?'

His readiness to share the blame was unexpected, and the touch of his hand too disturbing to be borne without some kind of response from her senses. Look-ing up at the dusky gold features softened by the lamp-light, she smiled.

'We'll both have to learn to count to ten!'

'To count to ten?'

It was so seldom that she could puzzle him, that she laughed delightedly when she saw his frown and shook her head. 'It's something Daddy used to say to me when I was letting my temper get the better of me. Hold your breath and let it out slowly while you count to ten —it's supposed to stop you losing your temper.'

'Ah! Then we shall both have to learn to count to ten, hmm?'

'I'll try.'

The black eyes scanned her for a second or two, and he smiled. 'I think we should celebrate your return home in some way. You would like that? When you are feeling quite well again.'

'Nuri——' She hesitated a moment, but then hurried on, praying he was amenable enough in this benevolent mood to receive the news of the dinner party his father was planning. 'Baba Refik has suggested giving a dinner party.'

'A dinner party? That is a good idea, you will like that, will you not?'

She neither confirmed nor denied her pleasure at the idea, because she was still in some doubt of her own feelings. 'He—he's quite anxious to meet Ian, having been told how much like Daddy he is.' Her voice had a light breathless sound and she realised suddenly how she was trembling. 'I've told him that Ian will be going home soon and he said we'll have the dinner party before he goes.'

It was obvious that something in her statement interested him very much and he was looking at her with slightly narrowed eyes. 'He is going home?'

'Very soon—in slightly less than a couple of weeks.'

'Ah!' It had to be satisfaction behind that short wordless exclamation, and for a second she felt the familiar flash of resentment. 'And Baba has decided that he will give a dinner party for him, hmm?'

'He said it would give him an opportunity to meet him.'

'Hmm!'

Laurette was left in some doubt as to what his opinion was at the moment, and she looked at him in mingled curiosity and anxiety. 'It was Baba Refik's idea, Nuri, and——'

'But of course—my father is entitled to invite whomever he pleases to his house, *bebek*.'

'Nuri, you wouldn't——'

A black brow swiftly elevated, cut her short, and she bit her lip. 'A guest in my father's house, Laurette? I imagine Baba has a certain curiosity about your cousin, it is natural enough in the circumstances. Also he is probably curious about his intentions.'

Laurette caught her breath, her lips parted in surprise as she looked at him. 'His—intentions?'

162

'Of course.' He got to his feet and stood for a moment looking down at her. She could have sworn there was a ghost of a smile lingering at the corners of his mouth when he reached down a hand to help her from her nest of cushions. 'It is customary in Baba's world for young men to call upon young women only when they have a betrothal in mind, and your cousin has called here on more than one occasion. It is possible that my father wishes to assure himself that this man's intentions towards you are honourable.'

'Oh, Nuri, no!'

He seemed to find her dismay amusing, for there was an uncharacteristic glitter of amusement in his black eyes as he looked down at her. 'Do you still shy away from the idea of marriage, *bebek*? Does it frighten you so much?'

'You have no right to talk to me about marriage, Nuri, you know that wouldn't please your father!'

His strong fingers tightened about hers in an inescapable grip and he held her where he could look down into her flushed face with a boldness that she was unaccustomed to and found shiveringly disturbing. 'But do you not wish to marry your redhaired cousin, eh?'

'I don't want to marry anyone!'

'Never?' His eyes taunted her, and she pulled helplessly at the hold he had on her. 'But surely you will not remain unmarried all your life?'

'If I want to, I will!'

With the hand he held he drew her towards him until she was aware of that tingling aura of masculinity about him that was something she had only lately become aware of. Looking down at her, he shook his head slowly, his black eyes unfathomable between those thick black lashes.

'I think not, *bebek*! Someone will make you change

your mind and you will go to him willingly!'

'You—you sound very certain about that!'

Her voice was breathlessly unsteady and she could do nothing about it, or about the trembling unsteadiness of her legs that felt as if they would not hold her for much longer. And Nuri smiled, a small but infinitely disturbing smile that gave his dark face a strangely satyr-like quality that sent shivers of sensation through her whole body.

'Oh, I am, *benim güzel*, I am very sure!' He bent his head for a second only and his lips touched hers with a lightness that promised so much that she closed her eyes instinctively in anticipation of a more passionate kiss. But while her senses still responded to the promise, he was once more looking down at her with those dark, unfathomable eyes and smiling. 'I think it is time for dinner,' he said. 'Shall we go?'

Her eyes wide and still slightly dazed, Laurette nodded. The strong fingers squeezed, drawing her towards the door, and she went unresistingly. At that moment she would have followed him anywhere.

Ian telephoned the following day to see how she was, and it was at Laurette's instigation that they arranged to go out somewhere, although Halet urged her anxiously not to go too far until she was well enough. It would be easier to issue Refik Kayaman's invitation to dinner on more neutral ground, she felt, where there was no likelihood of anyone witnessing his reaction. It was possible he would refuse, and she did not want Halet to be a witness to it if he did.

With the same concern as Halet, Ian refused to let her come any further than the end of the street, only a few metres from the house, and he was out of his seat and waiting for her when she appeared, seeing her into

164

the passenger seat of his car before he said anything at all.

Then turning in his seat he regarded her silently for a second or two before he leaned across and kissed her. 'How are you, love?'

Kissing her was a privilege he took for granted as her cousin, she supposed, but with Nuri's rather startling observations still fresh in her mind, she found it more unsettling than usual.

'I'm a lot better, Ian, thank you. I feel fine.'

'Headache gone?'

'Almost.'

He seemed undecided for a moment or two, then nodded suddenly, as if making up his mind. 'I think we'll just take a nice steady drive somewhere,' he decided. 'We needn't dash about, and you can stay out of the sun.'

His concern was touching, and she smiled at him as he started the car again. 'You're the one who has to keep out of the sun,' she reminded him. 'I'm used to it —it's only stone walls I tangle with.'

'Nevertheless,' Ian decreed firmly, 'we won't take any chances. I don't want your Turkish warriors breathing down my neck!'

'Ian, please!'

He sent her a brief grin over his shoulder. 'Sorry, love!' He shook his head, taking the car along the tree-lined street and down into the main part of Antalya. 'I just can't help feeling that your family of protectors must have me in mind for the villain after that little episode with the castle ruins.'

'Not at all!' Laurette thought of Nuri's frank opinion on the matter and for some reason smiled about it to herself. 'Nuri said he wouldn't dream of blaming anyone else when he knows I'm quite capable of doing something as daft as bumping into a wall and cracking my head.'

'Good God!'

Ian's stunned surprise made her laugh and she looked at his fresh, sunburned face for a moment while she brought herself round to issuing Refik Kayaman's invitation. 'In fact Baba Refik has asked me to invite you to a dinner party next week. Will you come?'

'A dinner party?' He looked as if he found it too incredible to believe. 'Are you serious?'

'Of course I'm serious, Ian!' She looked at him earnestly, hoping he was not making a vendetta of his feelings for the Kayaman family, and Nuri in particular. 'Baba Refik was a very good friend of Daddy's, 'an, and he—well, he would like to meet you for that reason anyway. I've told him how much like Daddy you are.'

'And that's his *only* reason?'

It wasn't going to be easy, and Nuri's implications last night about why his father wanted to meet Ian did not make things any easier when they kept popping into her mind every few minutes. 'I—I don't know that he has any other reason, except that you're my cousin, of course. The Turks are a very hospitable people, Ian, you must have found that, even in the short time you've been here.'

'Oh, I have! I get along well with most of the people I meet, but the Kayamans——' He shook his head, his face distorted for a moment into a grimace.

'Oh, Ian, you can't refuse! You can't possibly!'

'Code of manners and all that, you mean?' He looked as if he conceded the point, then nodded. 'O.K., cousin, never let it be said that I let the side down! I'll come to your dinner party, but just do one thing for me, will you?' Laurette frowned at him curiously and he grinned. 'Keep Nuri Bey out of my way, or I might let good

166

form go by the board and punch him!'

'Oh no, Ian, you wouldn't!'

From the stubbornly fierce look on his face it was clear that he would, given the provocation, and her heart fluttered uneasily. His blue eyes sparkled and he was grinning in a way she recognised as exactly like her father. 'Don't you believe it, love! I'd as soon punch that black-eyed devil as look at him, given half a chance!'

Laurette thought of Nuri and his antagonism towards Ian, just as fierce in its way and perhaps even more passionate when put to the test, and she wondered at two men disliking each other so much when they had met no more than three or four times at most.

'I don't understand you,' she said, watching his face curiously. 'How can you dislike a man so much when you scarcely know him?'

'Easy—when it's Nuri Bey!'

'But why, Ian?'

'I dunno.' He shrugged, grinning amiably at her over his shoulder. 'Maybe because I suspect he's got plans for you, and I hate the idea of you disappearing into a Turkish harem for the rest of your beautiful life!'

Laurette had said little during the past half-hour, and she thought Ian knew the reason behind her silence. He surely must realise how he had shaken her with that statement that Nuri had plans for her, though he had offered no further speculation on the subject, almost as if he realised he had said enough to make her uneasy.

They took a pleasantly steady drive as he had suggested, along the main motorway out of Alanya, eastwards out of the town, and Laurette gave her attention to the scenery whenever her preoccupation allowed it,

167

but always that disturbing suggestion of Ian's came back and distracted her.

He had kissed her, and being kissed by Nuri was a new enough experience to arouse her responses still when she remembered it. It stirred the kind of emotions in her that she had never thought herself capable of and it was quite unconscious when she touched her mouth lightly with her fingers.

Parked at the roadside at the edge of a village, she looked out at an olive grove, its squat, craggy grey trees sprawling on either side of them, like ungainly ghosts in the summer sunlight. A girl herding a flock of goats looked at them curiously from above the cloth carefully drawn across her face, questioning the fact of a man and a woman sitting in a car together, apparently without reason, thinking them lost, no doubt, but too shy to offer help without being asked.

The village houses straggled along a steep hill before them, surrounded and divided by orchards and fields of beans and wheat. It looked quiet and well ordered and as if it had not changed for a hundred years, which it probably hadn't to any degree. Laurette could find no fault with it, but she wondered if Ian shared her view, or even if he shared her view of very much at all, despite their relationship. He was still so much a stranger, and she was still much too unsure whether or not she wanted to remedy the fact in the short time available to them.

'You're quiet, cousin.'

Ian was smiling at her, half turned in his seat and with his bottom lip pinched thoughtfully between a thumb and forefinger. It was doubtful if he had any idea how much his seemingly casual remark had affected her, and she was probably taking it much too seriously, but somehow it was difficult not to.

'I'm thinking, that's all.'

'About coming back to England with me?'

She had forgotten about that, and her expression showed it as she hastily avoided his eyes. Looking out at the rolling countryside and the soaring impressiveness of the Taurus mountains she was reminded once more of how hard it would be to leave this country she had come to regard as her own, and it served to strengthen her resistance when she answered him.

'I hadn't really thought seriously about that, Ian. I —I hadn't thought about it at all.'

'I see!'

Clearly he saw her attitude as hostile and his blue eyes had a bright resentful look when she turned her head. 'Oh, Ian, please don't think I don't appreciate the fact that you offered to take me back with you——'

'But you just haven't bothered to give it another thought—I know! You probably prefer that damned harem after all!'

'And will you please stop talking such nonsense about harems! There haven't been any harems in Turkey for —for years! The Turks are a modern, civilised people and I won't have you always running them down just because you claim to be my cousin!'

'Claim?' He looked stunned for a moment, then one hand reached out and gripped around her upper arm, the fingers tight and digging into her flesh, as if he did not realise how hard he held her. 'Oh, you surely don't intend to deny it, not after this long?'

'No, of course not!' She shook her head, and found it aching far more than it had when she left home, so that she put a hand to her brow. 'I just wish you wouldn't always sound as if you dislike my family so much, that's all, Ian.'

'Do they know I want you to come home with me?'

She looked down at her hands rather than at him, and she wondered why she had been so reticent about telling Refik Kayaman at least. The old man had some inkling, she knew, he had more or less said as much, and so, she thought, had Nuri. They both suspected Ian of trying to lure her away, but she wondered what they would have said if they knew he had issued a firm invitation for her to go with him to England.

She shook her head, though it cost her a twinge of pain. 'I haven't said anything to them about it.'

Ian slid a hand beneath her chin and lifted her face, studying her for a moment or two before he spoke. 'Then I think you should, little cousin, don't you? Because I don't intend to let up, you know! I shall do everything I can to persuade you.'

'Ian——'

He leaned across and pressed his mouth to hers before she had time to say more, drawing her into his arms and holding her tightly, as if he feared she might try to pull away from him. But Laurette made no effort to resist, nor did she respond, and when he let her go at last, slowly and lingeringly, he was briefly puzzled but not deterred.

His mouth brushed her chin and the soft skin beside her ear, then pressed lightly to the vulnerable softness of her throat. It was an experience she would probably have found much more exciting only a week or two ago, but since then she had been held in Nuri's arms and he had kissed her in a way that took her breath away and made her tremble. She felt nothing like that when Ian kissed her.

Raising his head, Ian looked down at her with bright, determined blue eyes and smiled, one hand curved about her face as he lightly kissed her mouth again. 'I can be very persuasive,' he promised.

CHAPTER NINE

IT was because she sought reassurance about her foster-father's motive for giving a dinner-party and inviting Ian that Laurette sought Halet's opinion, but Halet had been disappointingly uncertain about it, so that once more she had been obliged to fall back on her own vague suspicions.

When Nuri had suggested that his father wished to meet Ian with a view to discovering his intentions towards her, she had not known whether to take him seriously or not, but further consideration had almost convinced her that it was likely.

Refik Kayaman took the whole man/woman relationship much more seriously than Ian probably realised, and she wondered if she ought perhaps to have given her cousin some warning hint. It was too late now, of course, for their guests would be arriving soon and Ian was probably already on his way, prepared to be formally polite, but still touchy and suspicious not only of his host, but particularly his host's son.

A glance at her watch showed her just how early she was, but she had been unable to settle as easily after lunch as Halet had, so she had come up to her room really much too early, and then spent more than half an hour soaking in a hot bath and trying to relax.

There would be several other people there as well, and it was silly to suppose that Ian's inclusion in the guest list had been prompted by any other reason than her foster-father's desire to meet the man who so closely resembled his old friend. Nuri's intimations had been meant to tease her, no more.

For a while she had pretty well convinced herself, while she lazed in the steaming luxury of the bathroom, but while she was dressing and doing her hair the uncertainties had returned. In a cloud of green chiffon and extravagantly perfumed to give her confidence, she whirled around in front of her bedroom mirror and watched her reflection thoughtfully. The colour suited her, and she felt very feminine in the flowing softness of chiffon, but the uncertainty she still felt showed to some degree, and she wished it didn't.

Ian was quick-tempered, but being so herself Laurette could hardly fault him for it. Nuri had quite frankly admitted to not liking him, and it was with both factors in mind that she foresaw an evening fraught with tension if the two of them were to be in frequent contact.

Nuri, she knew from experience, would and could hold his formidable temper in check rather than allow it rein against a guest in his father's house, but she wished she could be as sure of Ian's self-control. If he caused a scene that was likely to embarrass her foster-father she would find it very hard to forgive him.

'Oh, they mustn't, they mustn't!'

She murmured the words with her eyes closed and her hands close together under her chin. Then with one more rueful glance at her solemn faced reflection, she turned away, the chiffon dress floating romantically around her as she went.

There was no one else in the *salon* and it was a little too early for their guests to be arriving, so she sat on her favourite seat on the ottoman, skimming heedlessly through a magazine for a few minutes until she heard voices coming across the hall. Nuri and Halet, she recognised, and wondered what on earth they could be discussing with such feeling in their own tongue. It sounded very much as if they were disagreeing about something, and the suspicion was confirmed as soon as the door was opened.

Halet's darkly pretty face was flushed, and her eyes bright with the kind of resentment Laurette so often felt herself after an exchange with Nuri. He, of course, was well in control, although the black eyes glittered at her for a moment as he came across the room.

Half expecting to be involved, whether she wanted it or not, Laurette watched him cautiously, but all he did was murmur a greeting, then sit himself in one of the armchairs and pick up a newspaper. Halet, still flushed and looking unbelievably defiant, came and sat beside Laurette on the ottoman, her eyes quite plainly trying to convey a message.

Since she was unlikely to say anything while Nuri was within hearing, Laurette suggested they went for a walk in the garden before the guests arrived, a suggestion that Halet agreed to with such obvious eagerness that it was plain whatever she had on her mind she was anxious to share.

Nuri looked up, watching them over the edge of his newspaper as they rose together, and for a moment Laurette thought he had it in mind to say something about their departure. Instead he contented himself with a resigned shrug and disappeared again behind the newspaper.

Outside the air was cool and scented, and the gardens dappled by moonlight where the trees fluttered their branches in the breeze, the two of them walking side by side in silence for a few seconds, as if Halet sought

173

words to explain her secret. Then turning her huge dark eyes on Laurette, she sighed.

'I am sorry, Laurette, but the deception we had with the swim suit did not happen as we hoped it would.'

Momentarily caught unawares, Laurette frowned at her curiously. 'I don't quite understand, Halet.'

'You remember that I came to the hospital to collect that very bold costume that you had——'

'Oh, that!' Laurette already looked resigned. 'Is that what you and Nuri were talking about when you came in just now?'

Halet nodded. 'He has discovered about how little you wore when you went swimming with your cousin.'

'Oh dear!'

Halet's look suggested that she sympathised, but saw little hope of it being simply passed off. 'I am sorry, Laurette.'

'Why should you be?' Laurette smiled at her ruefully. 'You weren't wearing the blessed thing, I was!'

Halet pulled a face. 'He has also discovered that I went to the hospital to fetch it so that Baba—and Nuri —would not know about it.'

'Oh, Halet, no!'

'He has told me that to do such a thing was a deliberate deception and not worthy of me.'

Halet was quoting her brother, that was obvious, and the old familiar protectiveness for her stirred in Laurette for a moment. 'Oh, but he had no cause to scold you for it, you were trying to help me, and he should realise that.' Something else occurred to her then, and briefly cooled her indignation against Nuri. 'He won't have said anything to Baba Refik, that's one good thing.'

'Oh no, of course not!'

'But I shall tell him that he shouldn't have scolded

174

you for being loyal to me, that simply isn't fair!'

She would have gone and tackled him about it there and then, but Halet was pulling anxiously at her arm, and shaking her head. 'No, there is no need to do that, Laurette.'

'But he bullies you, Halet, you know he does!'

'I think not so much this time,' Halet argued quietly, and something in her manner made Laurette look at her curiously. 'I have admitted that I went to the hopital to fetch the costume because we did not wish them to know about it, but I have also told Nuri that it is not my concern what you choose to wear, nor the concern of anyone but yourself.'

Hardly believing her ears, Laurette stared at her for a moment. It simply was not like Halet to tackle her formidable brother with such home-truths, and she wondered where on earth she had found the nerve after all these years. She smiled, then eventually laughed, because she found it impossible not to, while Halet looked slightly sheepish with her eyes downcast and her cheeks flushed.

'I can hardly believe it, Halet! You, of all people! But what I don't understand is, how did Nuri *know*?'

Halet pulled a face, admitting herself a novice at deception. 'He guessed my reason for being so anxious to fetch your things when Doctor Alcilic told him at lunch time what you were wearing when you were taken to the hospital. He saw her with her husband and they laughed about how you could keep on such a brief costume while you were swimming.'

'Oh dear, he'd have hated that! I'd banked on the doctor being a bit more discreet!'

Halet regarded her for a moment. 'I think that Nuri is not so concerned that you were wearing the costume, but that you were with your cousin Ian when you were wearing it.' Her dark eyes had that curiously knowing innocence they sometimes did, and she was shaking her head. 'I am not always able to understand Nuri as well as Bedia and Latife do,' she confessed. 'He is behaving strangely.'

Refik Kayaman had referred to Nuri as being confused, and she had not followed his meaning, and now Halet was suggesting that there was something amiss with his behaviour too. 'Does anyone understand Nuri?' she asked, and Halet shrugged.

'I have defied him over your right to wear whatever swim suit you care to, and he is even more angry with me now—I understand that.'

'And I'm sorry about it, Halet. You got scolded for something you did for me.'

Always anxious about any form of rebellion, Halet looked at her for a moment, then shrugged. 'I *did* deceive Baba about my true reason for going to the hospital, but I have now shown Nuri that I too can be a rebel sometimes!'

'And now you're sorry?' Laurette pulled a face when Halet admitted it with a nod. 'I know the feeling, I get the same sense of remorse whenever I fight with Nuri. It's maddening, and it's even more maddening if he happens to be right!'

'I thought I should tell you.'

'In case he tackles me with it?' She hoped he was not going to, but she was already resigned to the fact that it was inevitable. Taking Halet's arm for mutual consolation, she laughed as they walked along the moonlit path. 'You won't know where you are after you're married, and you haven't got Nuri and me always around and fighting, will you, love? Just think how peaceful it will be!'

It would also be very lonely for a while for Laurette,

she realised, and Halet recognised it too. 'I shall miss you, my sister.'

That gently possessive title was even more than usually touching suddenly, and Laurette squeezed her arm reassuringly. It seemed much longer than eight years since she and Halet had become foster-sisters and confidantes, and she was going to miss her terribly, she knew. 'I shall miss you too, Halet.' She was surprised to find how choked she felt when she went to speak. 'We've had some good times together, haven't we?' She looked around at the scented trees and the waxy white blossoms of magnolia that brushed her arm with their coolness when she walked by them. 'I shall miss Yarev too, I've been happy here.'

'Oh, Laurette!'

It was clear that they could not go on in this vein without both breaking down in tears, and Laurette, as ever the leader, shook her head suddenly and smiled, determinedly cheerful. 'This is supposed to be a party,' she reminded Halet. 'We shan't look as if we're enjoying it much if we start crying our eyes out!' Glancing back over her shoulder at the house, she smiled ruefully. 'Let's go back, and give Nuri the chance to scold me and get it over with before the party starts.'

In fact she went back to the *salon* alone, for Hussein had arrived and met them in the garden, and with a tact that Nuri would probably have frowned on, Laurette left the two of them alone for a few moments. Hearing an arrival, Nuri was already on his feet and looked at her curiously when she came in.

'I thought I heard someone arrive.'

'You did, it was Hussein.' She knew he would question her being there in that case, but she had his disapproval of her and Halet still in mind and she perhaps sounded more defiant than she intended. 'I left them alone for a minute or two, it isn't often they have the opportunity for a bit of privacy, poor loves!'

Nuri's black eyes regarded her for a second or two, and she wished, yet again, that she could discover what was going on behind that implacable mask. 'And you do not approve of that?' he suggested softly.

She had meant to curl up on the ottoman, but somehow his standing there seemed to deter her, and instead she rested on one knee on the end of it and looked down at her hands as she turned the ring on her finger to catch the light.

'I sympathise with people who are in love as much as Halet and Hussein are and can't have a few minutes alone together sometimes.'

A hint of a smile touched Nuri's mouth, which she had to admit was unexpected, and he raised a brow. 'You understand the feelings of a lover so well?'

She was blushing, she realised, and it made her touchily defensive. 'I try! It's no longer considered promiscuous to hold hands with your fiancé, you know!'

'That sounds very much like your cousin talking, Laurette.'

'Well, at least Ian would understand my motives!'

It was happening again, and when she least wanted it to. He had shown no sign of anger until she goaded him to it, and now his eyes glittered with it, black and jet-like in those dusky gold features, while his strong, lean body was held firm and straight as a lance.

'I have little doubt that he knows you very well, *kizum*, since he has seen you almost naked!'

The colour flooded into her face, and there was nothing she could do about it, but the tears that suddenly blurred her sight of him were unexpected and she brushed them away impatiently. 'I *knew* you'd bring that up as soon as you had the opportunity!' she said in a small and breathless-sounding voice. 'You just couldn't resist it, could you, Nuri?'

His self-control, as always, stunned her, and even now when he was so obviously and violently angry, he managed somehow to control his voice until it was flat and harsh and quite unlike his normal tone. 'On the contrary,' he denied, 'I had not meant to say anything at all about it, and I despair of my weakness in allowing you to goad me!'

There were more voices in the hall suddenly, but Laurette scarcely noticed them. She cared for nothing but the fact that Nuri was furious with her for provoking him. He would not even have mentioned the wretched bikini if she had not provoked him into losing his temper for that brief second. She could have cried in her despair, but it was no time to let herself indulge in such self-recrimination when there were guests in the hall.

Guests or not, she couldn't face the whole evening knowing he was angry with her, and she made a tentative move towards appeasement. 'Nuri——'

'We have guests waiting!'

He turned swiftly and went striding away from her, then turned in the doorway and held it open for her. He would not give her the opportunity to say anything else, and it would be useless to try and persuade him now. She felt wretchedly unhappy, but she gave him one brief appealing glance then followed him across the room.

Walking past him, she kept her head down and tried not to be affected by that disturbing aura about him, more powerful than ever, she felt, at the moment, while he was so angry. He closed the door carefully behind her, then stepped forward to shake hands with the husband and wife who had just arrived.

179

Halet was with Hussein, alone in their own little world, despite the fact that there were other people around them, and Laurette felt suddenly and dismayingly alone. It was a feeling that Ian's arrival a few moments later did nothing to alleviate, although she felt somehow that it should have done.

Ian and Refik Kayaman had conversed quite a lot during dinner, and had apparently got on quite well together, but not once had Laurette seen him and Nuri speak to one another once they had exchanged formal greetings. Dinner over, she had come out into the garden with Ian, although they had said very little to one another so far.

A few steps along the path took them out of sight of the house where they were screened by a huge tamarisk that was sketched like a cluster of ostrich plumes against a moon-bright sky, and bringing them to a halt, Ian turned her to face him, looking down at her for a moment or two before he said anything.

'You aren't enjoying this party much, are you, love?'

It would be pointless to deny it, for her whole attitude gave away her mood, and she was in no mind to deceive him. Deception, however mild, had already caused her enough upset for one evening, and she shook her head.

'Oh, it isn't your fault,' she hastened to assure him when he raised a brow. 'I——' She shrugged resignedly when she was plagued once more by the stinging threat of tears. 'I had a row with Nuri just before the party started—it wasn't a very good start to the evening.'

'About me?'

She thought he sounded almost as if he hoped it had been about him and she shook her head firmly. 'No, about that wretched bikini!'

180

'Oh, for Pete's sake, Laurette!'

She smiled ruefully and caught at an azalea flower as she walked on a little way, twirling the blossom between her fingers. She did not look at him when he followed her but watched their shadows on the dappled path between the shrubs. Arguing with him was the last thing she wanted, and yet she saw little option if she stayed out here alone with him.

'It's a stupid thing to quarrel about, isn't it?'

'No, it isn't!' He brought her to a standstill, making sure she did not escape him this time by holding her hands firmly in his, his blue eyes glinting with determination. 'For God's sake, Laurette, tell him to go to hell and come home with me!'

'No!'

He held her firm against the sudden impulsive effort she made to free herself, and his mouth had a straight hard look that in some curious way reminded her of Nuri. 'Why not?'

She couldn't have explained, even had she wanted to, for her mood was unfamiliar, disturbing in some way she could not explain. All she was sure of was that she did not want to leave Yarev. Ian's fingers gripped her hard and he shook her lightly until she looked at him, her blue eyes big and almost fearful in the moonlight.

'Come with me, love. We could have a marvellous time together, I promise you.' Seeing that was not going to persuade her, he tacked off in another direction. 'You can't stay here, not while that devil keeps track of you like a——'

'No, Ian!'

Her heart was thudding hard and she felt oddly breathless suddenly as if she had run so hard and so long she had no strength left, and she was sure—all at once, she was sure why she did not want to go with Ian or anyone else who wanted to take her away from Yarev.

'I—I can't go away with you, Ian. Please don't make it difficult for me by insisting.'

'You're scared?' She shook her head slowly, still too dazed for the moment to realise how she was giving herself away, and Ian looked at her for a second with narrowed eyes, scanning her face with dawning realisation. 'Oh, ye gods and little fishes,' he breathed after a moment or two. 'So *that's* it!'

It seemed so quiet now that everyone had gone, and Laurette felt so bewildered by her own emotions that she could not even think of going to bed and sleeping. She was certain she would not sleep anyway, she had never felt more awake in her life, nor more confused.

Ian had been quick to recognise how she really felt about Nuri, but she prayed Nuri himself would not be so astute. It was quite possible that he found her attractive, his manner towards her once or twice lately suggested it, but he surely could not love her as she did him, and still be so critical of everything she did.

The rest of the evening had passed without her being aware of what was said or what was going on, she was only aware of Nuri's tall straight figure always somewhere in view it seemed, and always drawing her eyes irresistibly. He was with his father in the *salon* at the moment, and she hesitated to interrupt them to say goodnight, because they had seemed to be very serious about something when they went in there.

Halet had gone to bed a little while ago, leaving her in the garden alone, and she supposed she could quite easily go upstairs without saying anything to the two men. But old habits die hard, and she had never yet gone to bed without saying goodnight to her foster-father, she found it impossible to do so now. A brief glance round the edge of the *salon* door would suffice.

Crossing the hall, on tiptoe almost because the house was so silent, she tapped lightly on the *salon* door and opened it just a crack, a space big enough to put her head round. Nuri sat in one of the armchairs and he first looked up, sharply, as if he had been surprised, and then as hastily down at the floor between his feet.

Refik Kayaman occupied one end of the ottoman and he smiled, and waved her into the room, his voice soft and encouraging. 'Come in, *bebek*, *lütfen*!' Rather hesitantly she crossed the room, carefully avoiding a direct glance in Nuri's direction, and sat beside her foster-father on the ottoman, and the old man took her hands in his, his dark eyes looking at her for a moment musingly before he spoke.

'I—I came to say goodnight, Baba Refik—I didn't want to interrupt you.'

'There is little more to be discussed until I have spoken to you, little one.'

'Me?' Instinctively she glanced at Nuri, and found him watching her with a steady gaze that made her shiver involuntarily.

'I have met your cousin.' The old man was choosing his words carefully, and that somehow gave her a clue to the gist of them. 'He is very like my old friend, is he not?'

'Very much so, Baba.'

The dark eyes judged her reaction shrewdly. 'But you would not wish to marry him, I think, eh, *bebek*?'

'Oh no, Baba Refik, I've already told——' She caught Nuri's look from the corner of her eye and cut herself short hastily. 'No, I don't want to marry Ian, Baba Refik. For one thing because I haven't known him long enough—that's partly why I won't go home with him as he wants me to.'

183

'He has asked you to go with him?'

Refik Kayaman signalled his son to silence, but Nuri's black eyes still watched her and they glittered in the yellow lamplight as if he would like to have said a great deal more. 'I was not aware of this,' Refik Kayaman said, gently reproachful. 'You should have consulted me, *bebek*, it is not the kind of decision that you could have made on your own.'

'But I did,' Laurette told him, stating a simple fact. 'I told him I wouldn't go.'

'For that I am thankful.' The old man's hands held her gently and a slight pressure on her fingers made her look up at him. 'Are you still so firmly set against marriage, Laurette?'

Almost dizzy with surprise, she once more automatically and instinctively sought Nuri's eyes, then hastily lowered her own because she saw something there that disturbed her. Her heart was hammering so hard in her breast that she could scarcely breathe, and her mouth felt strangely dry so that she flicked her tongue across her parted lips before she answered him.

'It—it depends. I don't believe—I mean, I wouldn't just marry someone you—who was chosen *for* me.' She looked at the old man anxiously, still far too uncertain of what was happening. 'I couldn't let even you choose my husband for me, Baba, I just couldn't!'

'You disappoint me, little one.'

There was a smile on his lips, but a glimpse of anxiety in his eyes as he studied her was unexpected, and she watched him as he looked across at his son. 'It—it would very much depend on who it was you chose for me, Baba.'

The old man held her hands tightly, his face as benign as a bronze god in the lamplight. 'Would you consider my only son, my child?'

184

'Nuri!' She felt the colour that flooded into her cheeks and suddenly she felt like laughing and crying all at the same time as she clung tightly to the old man's hands. To Nuri himself she gave only a brief but telling look, that noticed the warmth in his black eyes and the smile that curved his wide straight mouth suddenly. 'Oh, yes, Baba, I'd marry Nuri—if he wants me to!'

From the armchair, Nuri's deep, quiet voice assured her. 'I have waited a very long time for you, my love, now I think I must wait no longer.'

'You should not be here!' his father told him with mock severity. 'In this instance I am the father of both the man and the woman, and it is a confusing role.'

'Oh yes, he should!' Laurette insisted, her voice soft and slightly breathless. 'You've observed your customs, Baba Refik, and I'd like to observe mine.' She did not look at Nuri while she said it, but at his father, a look of unmistakable appeal that was irresistible. 'Will you let Nuri ask me himself, Baba, just as he would if we were in England? It's—it's a custom I like, and it isn't as if Nuri and I have never been alone together.'

For a moment the old man looked at his son, then shrugged his broad shoulders and smiled as he got to his feet. 'It shall be so,' he agreed. 'I cannot deny you the right to your customs.'

'Thank you, Baba!' Impulsively she got to her feet and hugged the old man, planting a kiss on his cheek. 'You've always spoiled me, Nuri's often said so.'

'And now he will do so himself.' Refik Kayaman shook his head when she attempted to deny it. 'It will be so, now that he is sure of you, *bebek*, he need no longer fear that you will go away or that someone will come and take you away.'

He kissed her gently beside her mouth and gave a last look at Nuri, as if to warn him, then left them alone.

185

The silence in the softly lit *salon* after the door closed was almost tangible, and it was a second or two before Laurette felt the firm touch of strong hands on her arms turning her slowly round.

Nuri's black eyes looked down at her for a moment, deep and glowing as she had never seen them before, then he drew her close, pulling her into his arms, his face resting on the bright copper-red of her hair. Unsure at first, she laid her head on his chest, then slid her hands round behind him, across that broad back, until she pressed closer still and her whole being responded to the exciting nearness of him.

His mouth brushed her neck, lightly, like a promise, as he had done once before, only this time the promise was fulfilled. She lifted her face to him and his mouth covered hers, hard and fierce, yet strangely gentle too, while his hands moulded the softness of her to his own steely length. Brushing back the silky copper hair, he kissed her neck and the long fringe of lashes on her cheeks.

Looking up at last, Laurette studied the face that was at once so familiar and so new to her. Strong and dark, autocratic perhaps, but capable of gentleness, like the big hands that cradled her small flushed face between their warm palms.

'Have you really waited so long, Nuri?'

Her voice was light, breathless and barely audible, and Nuri looked at her steadily for a moment with those unfathomable black eyes. 'Since before you came back from school in Europe. Does that surprise you?' he challenged swiftly, when she looked startled. 'You were almost as lovely at sixteen and seventeen as you are now, my love, and I was man enough already to recognise it.'

'And yet you treated me as if you thought I was the most awful brat! You don't know how I hated you

186

sometimes. No,' she hastily amended something that she only now realised was not true, and never had been, 'I never hated you, however mean you were to me.'

'I was so afraid of losing you, and so afraid that you would realise how much I loved you, before you were old enough to accept the fact, that I perhaps—what is the phrase?—over-reacted.'

It seemed incredible, yet she had to know, and she looked up at him with none of the wariness that she had once felt, her blue eyes bright and curious. 'Is—is that why you've never married?'

Nuri laughed, then kissed her hard until she was breathless. 'If I tell you that, you will have all my secrets, my love! Be content to know that I have waited for four years for you, and now I have had to move quickly for fear Ian Kearn took you from me!'

She shook her head firmly. 'He couldn't have done!'

His mouth only a breath above hers, Nuri smiled slowly. 'But I did not know you had already told him you would not go with him. I was afraid he would sweep you off your feet and I should lose you for ever.'

'So you approached Baba in the recognised manner —the old way.'

'It is still our way, Laurette.' A hint of the old manner brought an anxious flutter to her heart. 'Do you not approve?'

Laurette buried her face against him, her voice muffled, but still quite audible. 'I approve of anything that makes it possible for me to marry you, my darling!'

Nuri lifted her face with one big hand and his black eyes were glitteringly bright as he searched her small face for his answer. 'Then will you marry me, my love?'

Through the window behind him the moon was riding high in a dark velvet sky and she smiled up at him again, her mouth already reaching up to him. 'I love you,' she said, and to Nuri that was answer enough.

Attention: Harlequin Collectors!

Collection Editions

of Harlequin Romances now available

We are proud to present a collection of the best-selling Harlequin Romances of recent years. This is a unique offer of 100 classics, lovingly reissued with beautifully designed new covers. No changes have been made to the original text. And the cost is only 95¢ each.

Not sold in stores, this series is available only from Harlequin Reader Service.

Send for FREE catalog!

Did you miss any of these exciting Harlequin Omnibus 3-in-1 volumes?

Anne Hampson

Anne Hampson #3
Heaven Is High (#1570)
Gold Is the Sunrise (#1595)
There Came a Tyrant (#1622)

Essie Summers

Essie Summers #6
The House on Gregor's Brae (#1535)
South Island Stowaway (#1564)
A Touch of Magic (#1702)

Margaret Way

Margaret Way #2
Summer Magic (#1571)
Ring of Jade (#1603)
Noonfire (#1687)

Margaret Malcolm

Margaret Malcolm #2
Marriage by Agreement (#1635)
The Faithful Rebel (#1664)
Sunshine on the Mountains (#1699)

Eleanor Farnes

Eleanor Farnes #2
A Castle in Spain (#1584)
The Valley of the Eagles (#1639)
A Serpent in Eden (#1662)

Kay Thorpe

Kay Thorpe
Curtain Call (#1504)
Sawdust Season (#1583)
Olive Island (#1661)

18 magnificent Omnibus volumes to choose from:

Betty Neels

Betty Neels #3
Tangled Autumn (#1569)
Wish with the Candles (#1593)
Victory for Victoria (#1625)

Violet Winspear

Violet Winspear #5
Raintree Valley (#1555)
Black Douglas (#1580)
The Pagan Island (#1616)

Anne Hampson

Anne Hampson #4
Isle of the Rainbows (#1646)
The Rebel Bride (#1672)
The Plantation Boss (#1678)

Margery Hilton

Margery Hilton
The Whispering Grove (#1501)
Dear Conquistador (#1610)
Frail Sanctuary (#1670)

Rachel Lindsay

Rachel Lindsay
Love and Lucy Granger (#1614)
Moonlight and Magic (#1648)
A Question of Marriage (#1667)

Jane Arbor

Jane Arbor #2
The Feathered Shaft (#1443)
Wildfire Quest (#1582)
The Flower on the Rock (#1665)

Great value in reading at $2.25 per volume

Joyce Dingwell

Joyce Dingwell #3
Red Ginger Blossom (#1633)
Wife to Sim (#1657)
The Pool of Pink Lilies (#1688)

Hilary Wilde

Hilary Wilde
The Golden Maze (#1624)
The Fire of Life (#1642)
The Impossible Dream (#1685)

Flora Kidd

Flora Kidd
If Love Be Love (#1640)
The Cave of the White Rose (#1663)
The Taming of Lisa (#1684)

Lucy Gillen

Lucy Gillen #2
Sweet Kate (#1649)
A Time Remembered (#1669)
Dangerous Stranger (#1683)

Gloria Bevan

Gloria Bevan
Beyond the Ranges (#1459)
Vineyard in a Valley (#1608)
The Frost and the Fire (#1682)

Jane Donnelly

Jane Donnelly
The Mill in the Meadow (#1592)
A Stranger Came (#1660)
The Long Shadow (#1681)

Complete and mail this coupon today!